THE
TRUE
ACTOR

THE
TRUE
ACTOR

Jacinto Lucas Pires

translated from the Portuguese by

Jaime Braz and Dean Thomas Ellis

DZANC
BOOKS

DIS|QUIET

1334 Woodbourne Street
Westland MI 48186
www.dzancbooks.org
www.disquietinternational.org

THE TRUE ACTOR

The True Actor was first published in Portuguese in 2011 © Jacinto Lucas Pires
e Edições Cotovia, Lda., Lisboa.

English Translation © Jaime Braz and Dean Thomas Ellis, 2013.

Published 2013 by Dzanc Books
Design by Steven Seighman
Edited by Jeff Parker

ISBN: 978-1-938604-48-5
First edition: November 2013

The publication of this book is made possible with support from the National Endowment for the Arts, the Michigan Council for Arts and Cultural Affairs, Direção-Geral do Livro dos Arquivos e das Bibliotecas, and Centro Nacional de Cultura.

Printed in the United States of America

10   9   8   7   6   5   4   3   2   1

THE
TRUE
ACTOR

1. Being Paul Giamatti

"Answer the phone," says the voice on the phone.

"But I'm already on the phone," says Americo.

"Five minutes. Answer the phone in five minutes."

"What if I'm still on the phone in five minutes?"

"You'll stand by the phone, and you won't move an inch, and you'll wait."

"Oh, really? And how do you know that?"

"I'm telling you, that's how. It's a very important call, so don't screw it up. Whatever happens, answer the fucking phone."

"All right, relax."

"Relax, nothing," says the voice. "Answer the phone."

"Got it," says Americo. "But right now I can't."

"All right, then, I'll hang up."

Five minutes later, the phone rings. Americo lets it ring three times and picks up. Murilo was right; it is a very important call. An English producer is on the line, a Somebody Summers, inviting him to play the lead in a big-budget international film, and soon. At first, Americo thinks that maybe this is some kind of joke, so he just goes "Uh-uh, uh-huh" whenever there's a pause on the other side, tentatively, so as not to commit himself. But he soon realizes, based on the lingo and his accent, that no, this is the real deal. It's too absurd to be a prank. He doesn't get half of what Mr. Summers says in his rapid-fire English, but this much is clear: the producer finds it incredibly funny that Americo works without an agent and the designated director of the film in question, the renowned Louis B. Kamp, deeply appreciated Americo's brutal turn as a drug lord in a detestable Spanish film that was shot in two-camera digital in less than a month and the production department urgently needs his e-mail address.

"You get what I'm saying? You got Internet, right?" Summers asks, carefully separating each syllable, as though Americo were a cave-dwelling troglodyte. Americo swallows hard, fakes a laugh, answers, yes, of course, and within seconds the script arrives on the computer. It is called *Being Paul Giamatti*.

As the title suggests, it's the story of Paul Giamatti, the character actor who made that amusing film about wine in America. *"Inspired,"* they write, in a note of introduction to the project, *"by the success of such diverse films as* Being John Malkovich *(Spike Jonze, 1999),* Synecdoche, New York *(Charlie Kaufman, 2008), and* Cold Souls *(Sophie Barthes, 2009), we now launch an exciting project,* Being Paul Giamatti *(working title). We call it a 'non-sequel,' and in it we conjure everything that has and hasn't been conjured, every possible (and imaginary) reference to history and fiction, everything that has ever existed and everything that hasn't, all in an unprecedented attempt to create the very first human being made purely from moving images and Dolby Surround sound."* It is, of course, the story of a fictional Giamatti as the character in a bizarre video game called *Being Alive*. The story of Giamatti as a stranger in the world, an unwitting poet and an adorable schlump. The story of Giamatti as the happy-sad clown. More or less.

The film begins in one of those seedy bars where the velvet curtains have suspicious stains and amateurs of all kinds are permitted, encouraged even, to step up onstage (for no remuneration whatsoever) and tell a few jokes, sing, dance, make political statements, declare their abiding passions, confess their sins—that kind of dive. Paul Giamatti (that is, Americo, the actor playing him) sits at a table with a platinum blond, older than him and resoundingly, thunderously fat. On stage, a girl dressed, let's say, like Cleopatra performs a reasonably rhythmic number with a fiddle, two boxes of matches, a remote-controlled chicken and a book of poetry, when, at a certain point, the blond says to Giamatti, "What are we drinking, Baby?"

Giamatti smiles, nods, and summons the waiter. "Champagne!" he shouts, and sneaks a glance to check her reaction. But the confounded blob only has eyes for the chicken, running hysterically around the flaming book of poetry as the half-naked Cleopatra tears the pages into shreds and lights them on fire, wielding the fiddle in a kind of absurdist calisthenics.

By the time the bottle of champagne is empty, a guy in a white shirt and black bow tie is behind the microphone. He looks like a boxing referee but speaks in an unbroken string of non sequiturs: "Politicians get a bad rap," "Sports are fine with me, but then again they're not," and "Once I went to Italy, then I went to Oklahoma." It's your typically lame stand-up comedy act, the kind that always falls flat. Well, maybe not typical-typical. It lacks the grievous, deadweight silence following each joke, that strange empty echo that heightens the tiny disreputable noises that normally go unnoticed. In this case the people simply stop listening. The crowd gets distracted, talks in asides to each other, turns back to the bar and to their drinks, focuses their attention inward, and the meek little voice of the boxing ref lapses, diminishes, drowns. "An ass from here to the Himalayas," are the last words Giamatti hears from the stage before the blond whispers, "I gotta go to the shit house," and coarsely swings her majestic rump around the tables and disappears. It's an expression he loathes, "the shit house"; it bugs the hell out of him, leaves him in a foul mood. Now he is alone, looking up at the stage. How sad. Well, not sad, exactly, sad is nothing. Pathetic, ponderous, pusillanimous.

Suddenly he becomes intensely conscious of every gesture, each banal occurrence in his body, the noises in his belly, the itching in his inner ear. He doesn't know where to put his hands. His fucking hands, now a problem of practicality. He tries various positions: right on top of left, like a shell; both with fingers open and joined, like a crest; and one on either side, above the table, in "death mode." But nothing helps, of course, no position works; it's just a way of killing time.

Onstage the boxing ref, pale and nervous, defeated by the fierce indifference of the crowd, interrupts to say: "Well now, I ...." An amusing grimace appears on his face, like he's just tasted a bitter inedible fruit, and he exits, almost runs, staggering out like an untethered marionette. Not looking where he walks, he gets tangled in the curtains and stumbles out of sight. No one notices. For two, three astonishing minutes his foot remains visible from the side of the stage. It can even be seen from the edge of the curtain. The shoe-leather, a terrible, translucent brown, remains visible for two, three long minutes, until the ref departs for good. He carefully gathers his foot with a sort of vague disgust, as if he were picking up a banana peel from the floor to toss in the nearest trash can. From the stage the foot—*zap!*—vanishes.

The crowd has quieted. They look at each other, unsure what this all means, and then they burst into laughter and applause: "Bravo! Encore! Encore!" The blond never returns.

The plot unfolds a bit after this opening scene. Then other adventures, other complications, new layers. This is an *auteur's* film; it's got a certain degree of complexity.

Holding the script in his hands, the pages freshly printed and freshly read, Americo is content but a little in shock. The invitation to act in a serious film has come at just the right time. For six months now, nine counting the holidays, he has been out of work, with no offers coming his way: no plays, no soaps, no dubbing gigs, not one lousy commercial. (And how can you count holidays if you're out of work, holidays from what?) Day after day spent at home taking care of Joachim, now a year and seven months, constantly crying, screaming, falling down, messing up, breaking things, putting stuff in his mouth, choking, coming down with fever, taking medicine, getting vaccinated, sleeping little and crying and screaming and dirtying diaper after diaper that Americo, sooner or later, has to change, since, during the day, he's the only adult in the house. In his spare time he works on his own ideas, he won't resign himself, he will not, he will *not* allow himself to be, as a soap opera character he played some years ago put it, *crushed by the fatal grinding gears of this world.*

Recently he's been thinking of a project he can offer to the National Theatre Association for Portuguese Production. He doesn't yet have a script or a title, but he does have some clues as to format, style, and overall tone. A one-man touring show in the popular vein, intelligent yet commercial, entertaining yet profound. Well, profound *enough*, anyway. The idea is to take the soliloquies from Shakespeare's Falstaff and to cleverly reassemble them, cutting and pasting and such, teasing out their underlying meanings, and draping it all in a lighter, more jocular cloak, a little nonsense, and then a finale that leaves no doubt as to when it's time to applaud, an ending that feels like an ending, an ending that is assuredly final. Yet meanwhile it lacks a metaphor. And this is how the theatre works. You must find a metaphor that connects everything and justifies everything. Maybe dress Falstaff up as Secretary of State. This idea occurred to him just the other day during one of his rare moments of solitude, in the bathroom. But he's still not sure about it. He needs to think it all through a bit, there is still much work ahead.

Joana tells him he's not being realistic, that he's never realistic, that such an idea is utterly without merit. "Falstaff?" she says, as though it were a novelty, a joke, a minor malady.

"My dear Americo, no promoter in any theatre in the country is going to buy a show that features a, what's he called again, 'Falstaff'? ... Ha, ha."

"But he's a famous character."

"Oh, come on. Be serious."

"And it's … Shakespeare."

"Shakespeare? Shakes-*peare*? My dear, that's even worse!"

"Please don't say 'my dear' like that."

"You've got two obscure names instead of one."

"Really? You think so?"

"Yes, I do, Americo. I do."

"Perhaps," he says, just to end the conversation. "Maybe I'll have to sell the idea without mentioning it comes from the Falstaff … of Shakespeare."

"Yes, I think that might be best. My dear."

And the way she utters those two words, without looking at him, as if he were some kind of lackey, there just to watch her house, to babysit her child, as if he were an odious joke for this great and successful woman to stomp on with the stylish heel of her shiny-fine Italian shoe, the way she says these words at this moment makes him detest her with such an intense violence that Americo tells himself there is only one resolution. "Oh, my dear Joana, when you talk to me this way … well, wow, wow. And well, what if—now that the kid's asleep and all—what if, if we, um, go … you know. Just to unwind a bit … what do ya think?"

"Tonight," she says, in a professional, neutral tone, utterly devoid of malice, "Tonight I have work to do."

She is the quintessential modern woman, hardworking and successful. At thirty, she's reached the top or very near the top of the civil service and is nothing less than the Deputy Assistant to the Regional-General Subdirector of the National Department of Quality Control of Olive Oil and Oil Mills, the youngest woman to hold such a position, with excellent prospects for career advancement, due to her high marks in both external and internal Service assessments, and whenever there is an important study to be done, or whenever an opinion is required on a weighty or delicate matter, it is she who management trusts to, shall we say, "tie up loose ends." This requires lots of homework on the part of the young, high-level bureaucrat, night after night reading dossier after dossier, document after document, reports and analyses and letters and files and articles and recommendations, etc; etc., ad infinitum. At night Americo goes to the bathroom and, when he comes back to bed, his wife is asleep, snoring open-mouthed. The usual routine. How endearing, that kind of childlike expression that certain people have when they sleep. Her blond hair pleated perfectly into the pillow, her delicate eyelids smooth as plastic.

In bed Americo opens the book he's been reading for over a month. *The Expletive*, by Eduardo Fontes. A curious and quite intriguing novel, it's the story of a woman who lives "outside of language" and can only get inside words, only divine their essence, through violent acts against others and against herself. It's not easy, after such a tiring day, and with such a demanding book, to stick to his self-imposed obligation to read at least ten pages a day. The thing is not to lapse into the indolent melancholy of the idler who only changes diapers and does housework and has no other interests, a clueless dolt with no original ideas, no desires, no authentic joy.

This time, to be truthful, he doesn't even make it halfway. He falls asleep on the second sentence of the first paragraph of the third page: "Carmen was thrilled with the cadence of more complex clauses; meanwhile, if someone said 'dog' or 'building,' she found that she could not conjure an image to fit the word."

With this in mind, he dreams of a white place where things only materialize if someone names them and thinks of them at length. A kind of postmodern asylum, where Americo sits on the floor looking into the void, trying to block his thoughts, terrified that he might spawn, in this forced damnation, some malevolent word that will create, in turn, something equally evil, and real. What's even worse is that this is not exactly a nightmare. Americo has no cold sweats, nor does he wake up screaming, "Mother!"

But in the morning he is stricken with a generic malaise that will, no doubt, stick with him all day long. He'd prefer any fever whatsoever to this bizarre lethargy that lets him see everything as though it has already occurred, everything dispassionately blighted and empty. He turns on the television and sits down with Joachim to watch the news. His wife has already gone off to her olive oils, it's now an all-male household. Americo couldn't care less, obviously, about the news, he just needs something to do, some place to look, some fast-moving images.

There are "insurrections" in two or three "problem neighborhoods," but the government spokesman says there is no cause for alarm. On the other hand, representatives of the opposition are exhibiting their outrage and speaking in overlong sentences in which the word "social" and the word "security" are repeated over and over again. Joachim finds this amusing, and stretches his arms in the direction of the television.

Then he starts crying.

"It's all right, today it's okay," says his father, and Joachim calms down. He lets him knock his forehead against the TV screen. Perhaps this is bad for him, but it's an understandable impulse and Americo doesn't want him flying into a tantrum from all the lunacy. And also it's good for the kid to learn some things on his own, from his own mistakes, let him smash against the hard screen once in a while to realize that images are just images and have nothing to do with reality. His son's silhouette is framed against the Afghan landscape when his cell phone suddenly vibrates.

XXX?

It's her. A text message. She always writes him in this primary code; he doesn't know why. If someone were to hack into his cell phone, this would be the most suspicious message of all. Maybe she means it as kind of a joke. As if this agreement between them had even a trace of levity. A game, a fantasy of spies, thieves, secret agents. Or maybe she doesn't know how to text or is afraid of making spelling mistakes—not that she's an idiot, quite the contrary. She's one of the most intelligent people Americo has ever known. Not a cultured intelligence but a singularly refined one: a touch of malice, an instinct for the perfect turn of phrase, an astonishing ability to argue wordlessly, to win disputes with just a look or the way she closes her mouth. The sting she delivers with every pause, every silence, fuck, just thinking of this puts Americo all out of sorts. *Be there in 30,* he texts. Then he calls his mother and invents a story about some impending deadline at the Finance and Social Security office and a hell of a fine if he doesn't show up and would she do him this huge favor and, not to worry, the boy will just sleep quietly the whole time and won't wake up for another two or three hours, and his mother says okay, as soon as she finishes her lunch she'll come over the house and watch "Baby Joachim."

"Mother, please."

"*Joachim*, then. Just kidding."

Half an hour later, Americo crosses the garden of Pleasure Plaza, a decrepit spot right out of a dream—giant, twisted trees, exposed black roots—and it feels as if all his blood is flowing from his chest to his arms and from his arms to his hands, all pulsing with the desire to embrace this woman.

The pension has no name, no signboard outside. Americo tells the bald woman at the front desk that there's "someone" waiting for him in Room Six and the woman tilts her head toward the staircase.

"Americo," she says, as she opens the door.

"Carla …," he says, "Bruna." It is a shock just to see her. She's a difficult woman to fully recall, a surprise of a woman who always makes his adrenaline shoot to dangerous levels. Up close, facing her, Americo is afraid he might swoon like one of those nineteenth-century romantics. This Carla Bruna is infinite, eternal, begin where you will—the evil eyes, the great lips, the naked neck, that white mark in the slope of her buttock. Her tawny aroma enters you through the mouth, the skin, stays with you as if from another realm; your brain swells with a better, cleaner oxygen. Life is so much easier to understand this way: a thing you can touch, grab hold of, turn inside out, ahh. Americo is no wimp, far from it, but one time after leaving her room he was given to poetry. It went like this: *Carla Carla Carla Carla / Don't you know that you're my Bruna / This killing thing that you possess / How pure, this sweet distress!* He can't remember the rest, but it wasn't half-bad and it rhymed until the end. He never showed it to her, of course, they weren't as complicated as all that, commitments and endearments. She asks nothing from him, and he gives her only what he gives her and only when he feels like it. Every now and then she sends him a text, *XXX?*, always the same, *XXX?*, and that's that.

After their rendezvous in Room Six of the Pleasure Plaza, he leaves some cash folded under the bedside lamp, and that's that.

Not that she has ever asked for money. Nor does he feel obligated, things being as they are, she being Carla Bruna, the *grande dame* of the nocturnal Lisbon underworld, and he being, well, just him. No, he doesn't feel the least bit like her client. He leaves the banknotes, tucked into the base of the brass lamp, half-hidden, with the utmost regard, just because. Because he truly likes her and because he knows she needs it, it'll make things easier for her. It's just a little bit of cash. A token gesture. Her work at Club Erox is, he suspects, poorly paid and irregular and provides her no guarantees whatsoever.

When he gets home his mother, retired for a year now from her intermediate position in an insurance company, is watching a disaster flick from the '70s with her grandson on her lap. A virus, transmitted purely by sight, bodies inexplicably exploding.

"Isn't that a little violent for him?"

"He's still too young to get it. So, did you manage to resolve everything?"

"Um, well," says Americo, "one never manages to resolve *everything. ...*"

And, hearing this, his mother—does she suspect something?—allows herself just a slight, Mona Lisa-like, smile.

2. Full Name

The next day Americo heads straight for the Office of Finance and Social Security. If he wants to collect his sweet sum from the film *Being Paul Giamatti*, he must return to Active Status. This is a serious, *professional* production, and these serious, *professional* types won't pay without a receipt, and in order to get a receipt, well, one needs to attain Active Status; and so he summons the courage to show up.

He takes Joachim along in his stroller so he can get "priority treatment" and move to the head of the line at Public Services. It's a great little scheme that falls just short of a swindle. The boy is, after all, his son, and he is the boy's father and that's the way the world works. Besides, Joachim doesn't mind one bit; in fact, he even likes it. He's got a pacifier in his mouth and, in an open-eyed dream, his face reacts to every detail of the city: all its colors, all its houses, all its giant toys.

"Full name."

"Americo Santos Sousa Silva Abril."

A woman with short hair and dismissive gray eyes hands him a sheet of paper. It's an A4, full of squares and lines just like in one of your more contemporary sketches. In order to "return to Active Status," she explains, he must first complete the form stating who he is, list the ID numbers of all his city- and state-related documents, his current address, occupation, marital status, domicile, level of education completed, annual income, capital gains estimate for the current fiscal year, all other sources of income, and which, if any, professional associations he may belong to, any debt he may owe to any public agency, and if so, whether it is small or medium or scandalous, if he spends much time abroad and where, if he has ever held any public position, whether he prefers the beach or the countryside, men or women, prose or poetry, opera or football, Pessoa or Camões, Eusébio or Amália, and on what day of what year he "left active status" (print in Portuguese in capital letters and write legibly, please).

At noon, as agreed, he meets with Murilo and Andrade-Pinto at Pinocchio Cafe. By the time he arrives, pushing his son in the stroller, they are already on their second Imperial. "This is my last beer," says Andrade-Pinto. "I have to go back to work."

"Are you serious?" says Americo, astounded, "Where?"

Andrade-Pinto lets out a laugh. "A toast to the geeks of the world!"

"Quiet, you'll wake him."

"Dr. Andrade-Pinto, did you hear that?" says Murilo. "You'll wake up little Joachim."

Murilo is a friend from childhood, the only one from those days with whom Americo is still in touch. He has a long, yellow-brown face, with permanent dark circles around the eyes. He's a lawyer, but he says, with studied embarrassment whenever the subject comes up, "Yes, well, only in my spare time."

"So the little shit's name is Joachim?" asks Andrade-Pinto.

Andrade-Pinto is something else. He lives off his wife, a dermatologist at one of the country's best clinics, and considers himself to have an artistic temperament. He takes some photographs every now and then, always looking to "work with the light" on "themes of an abstract nature." He turns towards Americo, eyeing him over the rims of his dark glasses. "You said Joachim, is that right?"

"Yes, I did. Why?"

"Oh, nothing."

The boy snores in the stroller. He may be little, but what style: he vogues like a hybrid of gangster and fado crooner, pacifier tucked into the corner of his mouth, nose upturned, a general air of cockiness on his face. Even asleep, he puts everyone on alert, the little motherfucker.

"And who came up with the name?" asks Andrade-Pinto.

"Joachim?" asks Americo.

"Who do you think?" asks Murilo.

"You're asking me?" asks Americo.

"You're asking me?" asks Andrade-Pinto.

Murilo keeps quiet, takes another swig of beer. He smiles, as it were, to himself.

"She did," Americo replies. "Joana picked the name."

And with this evil utterance—the word "Joana," the word "she"—a weighty silence falls upon the table. They no longer look at each other, and dare not speak, grace be to God, another word. They all turn to face the plaza and quietly watch the procession of cars on the Restauradores.

Not that this is a bad outcome, mind you, what with the silence and the beers.

On the way home, Americo buys a newspaper with a picture of "the international superstar arriving on these shores to put on a performance not to be missed." He folds it carefully, tucks it under his arm. He's wearing a short-sleeved shirt, and the singer's face grazes, ever-so-lightly, the inner part of his elbow. And what a tender face it is. But he keeps his cool, refuses to allow himself to get carried away by the hoopla. He puts on a serious face and keeps walking. He will not ogle the woman's photo in a public plaza, in front of all these people; this he will not do.

He arrives home in a sweat, exhausted from pushing his son's stroller up one street and down another, then back up another. What a day, the sun-in-a-surreal-sky kind of day. He shuts the door and props himself against the wall to restore his equilibrium. He exhales, he inhales. Christ, he's not twenty anymore. His son regards him with amazement from the stroller, as though breathing itself were a work of art. "It's all right," Americo says. It occurs to him that his son is growing way too fast, and has gotten fat; his weight seems a sudden, ridiculous thing. He loosens the straps that hold him in the stroller and sets him on the floor. "Get a move on," he says.

Joachim looks at him with those big animé eyes, bursting with life.

"Get going," he says again. He nudges him forward with his hands, as though he were shooing a fly. "You're on your own, you're free, go to your things, go."

The kid doesn't budge.

"All right then, do as you please," he says, at last, feigning indifference, and sits down on the couch to read the newspaper.

It's all one big letdown. Inside there's nothing but a ridiculous little mention of the superstar's tour and a photo of the woman leaving Portela airport, dressed up to her ears from the bitter cold; what nonsense. The other news is a bunch of depressing claptrap about the state of the nation and the mounting tensions in all its sectors: the economy, education, health, justice, security, the arts. Groups of the unemployed have begun to organize into autonomous "pressure groups" threatening "new forms of protest" and a "more literal" call to arms. Around the province, discontented teachers on hunger strikes in front of schools wield banners with revolutionary slogans and didactic posters with diagrams of entrails and digestive organs. Judges in their robes outside the courthouses chant their demands in Latin: better working conditions, better legislation, greater respect. Americo no longer understands what's going on; suddenly it's as if this is all happening in another country, in a place he doesn't recognize, on some black-and-white street, where an angry mob, fed up with everything, is streaming past. An immense mob in an orderly Portuguese fury, calling out names left and right, Americo not knowing whether to put his hands in his pockets or fold his arms across his chest or what, not knowing what kind of face to put on, a nice condescending smile or the stern mask of one who thinks and doubts, Americo stuck in the middle of that vast, streaming crowd and feeling more and more alone, more and more like a stranger. He looks up at the flowers in the trees, the marvelous jacaranda flowers, and wants to point them out to all those passing by, "Look, how pretty ...," but no one stops, no one listens. A multitude united by the force of a *NO*. An impervious, nay-saying mass constructed of headlines and sound bites, people rancid with real life, still soiled, smudged with the black dust of newsprint, as if they have just fled a war zone, a catastrophe, the wreckage of a decimated city. Americo, with a mix of fear and fascination, leans against a tree trunk as the crowd surges past. They march at a rapid, insistent pace, following a forceful cadence. He hears—by the hundreds, by the thousands— their simultaneous footsteps on the pavement. People who rob gas stations, ATM's, jewelry stores in order to have something to eat, people who want a home or just some time to spend there, people black with angst or white with fright or brown with doubt; he has no idea from where they've all come, occupying the streets and the avenues with their familial battalions, with their diverse odors (odors in which the city and the country converge, a bizarre mix of generic soaps and roadside vegetation), people who rob drugstores to get medicine for their children and people who rob pharmacies to shoot themselves up with aspirin powder, people who've come from spacious continents to live in crowded slums, young and beautiful and perfectly lost people, with no future in sight, with nothing to wish for, people dressed in an incongruous mix of colors, people who, by the way they walk and the faces they wear, quickly reveal a diversity of culture and tradition, giving off the light of another time, and he leans against the tree trunk and watches them pass. Such strange faces, such strange bodies. He wants to speak to them of Beauty, show them those lovely jacaranda flowers, the heartrending beauty of their lilacs against the blue sky of Lisbon, he wants to touch them with this, allow them this rapture, anything that could bring even a fleeting smile to their lips, but it's hopeless, it won't work, no one pays him any mind. All the reckoning from that clamorous *NO* has blinded them to everything else; it's useless. As if anything has ever come from a *NO*. On the black-and-white street, along the big abstract boulevard that leads to the House of Parliament, Americo Abril holds himself against the jacaranda tree and marvels at the faces—foreign and suburban, poor and middle-class—a streaming chorus of "No! No! No!" while the lilac petals rain down and gradually he hears the piercing cries of his son. "What is it?" he says, and closes the newspaper.

Joachim, of course, doesn't respond. He still doesn't know how to speak, only how to shriek and cry, sometimes simultaneously.

"Don't cry," says his father. "All right then, go ahead, cry, no, stop ..."

But the boy won't stop howling. Eyes shut tight, mouth wide open, an expression that recalls the old roller coaster at Entrecampos. Could he be hungry, perhaps?

Americo microwaves the plate of green baby food that Joana left prepared in the fridge. The big moment approaches—getting the kid to taste it. He sits him in his high chair, struggles to tie the plastic bib around his neck. The moment of truth has arrived: feeding time.

Joachim begins to squawk the second he sees the slop on his plate.

"Look, dude, I can relate. I'd scream, too, if someone tried to feed me this crap." Americo speaks softly, in a jovial, childlike manner, so his son won't pick up exactly what he's saying. Not that he understands many words, but one never knows. He takes a spoonful of the green-white gruel, blows on it to cool a little so the boy won't burn himself, then, very slowly, theatrically, trying to divert his son's attention and stop him from screaming, lifts the spoon in the direction of his mouth. "Here comes the little airplane ..."

And just as the spoonful of mush passes through the parted lips of his immense mouth, Joachim—beloved little offspring, pride of his father—eyes bugged in an expression of dubious, eternal expectation—*Ptui!*—spits it all out. Shit, fuck. Americo is completely soiled—fuck!—his designer shirt covered with mouthfuls of green slop, as is the floor and the Afghan rug that Joana bought on the Internet.

The boy screams even louder.

"Eat!" commands Americo. "You hear me? You've got to eat!"

But his son is unmoved. He cries even louder, bangs his hands against the tray of the high chair, forces the blood up to his face, and unleashes a fresh, even more piercing, series of shrieks, an outburst that busts some cord in his father's temporal lobes, an unimaginable agony. "I give up …," Americo groans.

Still the boy won't shut up, not even close. He screeches with an inhuman, savage indifference. His son is as uncivilized as the beasts of the caves, the forests, the primeval nights.

Americo rises, his fist clenched. He wants one thing only: to hit the kid. Just a little tap, mind you, enough to see if it'll shut his trap, teach him a little etiquette. But of course he won't; after all, the little shit's not even two. He lets his hand fall and swallows it all in.

The boy keeps crying; pure torture.

Americo turns away from him and goes to the window. He imagines that all his pain is coming from a hemorrhaging inner ear. He must be on the verge of madness, the point of no return. He sees his son wasting away, day by day, hour by hour, his mouth shut tight, tight, tight. His son, nasty as a cobra, beloved above all else. His arms and legs like toothpicks, the ribs protruding, the bones in his face and his skull almost visible, the eyes dislodged from their sockets. He sees disease, despondency, death, the void, dear Jesusgod. "Joachim, open your mouth!"

The boy refuses.

"Joachim, listen to your father! This is an order!"

No, he'll have to try it another way. He scratches his head, looks at his distraught offspring. But what way, how? The way of delicacy, of love, of gentleness and understanding?

Tentatively he approaches his son, lowers himself to the level of his eyes and, with his knees pressed against the cold floor, tells him the story of the Death Child, a walking skeleton with dark circles under the eyes that reached the floor and who spoke in a language of only consonants—"wrtpsfghjlkçzxcbnm"—who drooled yellow spittle from the corners of his mouth and frightened all children. He tells him of a dystopian Lisbon, one of purple skies, honeycombed houses, and families afraid to look at each other on the street. People who won't look up so as to not be snatched by some nameless monster. "One fine day the Death Child walks to the center of town and do you know what happens?" Now, at last, he listens. Ah, yes; mesmerized, he listens to the horror story that this actor invents, and eats with utter elation the green mush that Mommy made for Daddy to give him. He devours all of it, right down to the last disgusting drop.

3. This is Magnificent

Joana is a gem when she wants to be and a sweetheart when she can be, and she cuts quite an upright and elegant posture at whatever dinner table she sits. Here she is at the Rodrigues', chatting animatedly with the hostess, Mariana Rodrigues, about diapers, canning jars, and baby creams. And clothes and baby wear and vaccines and zits and bibs and breast pumps. It's too much for him. Americo looks over at Mario Rodrigues for some complicity, a little conspiratorial comfort, but his friend doesn't seem the least bit fazed by the conversation. He's got a pleasant, vacuous grin on his face.

With nothing to say, Americo turns his attention to his plate. The punched potatoes are excellent. "This is ... magnificent," he says.

But he may as well be at the bottom of a mine shaft in some imaginary desert.

This is a curious mystery indeed. The notion that punching a food could alter its flavor seems absurd—yet here it is. After being punched the potato discovers its secret personality, its tipping point, its calling, so to speak. Suddenly its complex nature is revealed, a sophisticated framework of flavor, aroma, color, texture, consistency and form, a complexity we would never suspect when contemplating the banal tuber in the red netting that we bring home from the supermarket. It's something that can only be understood empirically: take an unpeeled potato, roast it the amount of minutes that tradition requires, then stick it with a good punch. A forceful but restrained wallop, gallant yet gentle. A miracle is guaranteed. Suddenly, right before our very eyes, a brand new potato, at once hard and soft, assertive and submissive, compact and obliging. A potato just like the savory ones on the Rodrigues' Nordic china. An endearment of a potato: the surprising crunch of the skin contrasting marvelously with the anticipated softness of the inside, the smooth surface of the knife blade slicing so convivially into its porous heart, gently giving way to receive the olive oil and garlic. Ohh. Ahh. On the side, a piece of codfish cut into a rectangle, none too thick, with just the right amount of salt, the ideal happy medium—so difficult to achieve—between "merely salty" and "too salty." And, topping it all off, the *pièce de résistance*—the garlic-infused olive oil. Wow. A flavor that makes one think of old times, of twilight, cities in flames, dark-skinned people, deep wrinkles, and other such images. But Americo won't go there. It would take a serious, truly talented lyric poet to properly conjure such mysteries. And besides, one shouldn't talk with food in in one's mouth.

"They have the tiniest little socks and shoes there, so precious, you can't imagine," says Joaninha.

"Oh really, where?" asks Mariana. "Would you take me there sometime, tomorrow, perhaps?"

When her husband Mario hears this he says nothing. Does nothing. He sits in the exact same position, with that dim, benevolent smile on his face. Could the guy be on meds?

They've known each other, the four of them, for fifteen years. Once, for no particular reason other than to give their leisure-time gatherings for small talk the status of a formal organization, they christened themselves The Nothing. They would say to each other: "Don't forget today's meeting of The Nothing," or "The Nothing meets tomorrow night at the King Cinema to see the new Jarmusch." They believed they were going to create resounding revolutions, masterwork modes of living; they envisioned themselves eternally free of the conventions of their parents and grandparents, believed they would live together forever, constructing "a true, quotidian utopia of free love," much "truer" and much more in line with the "thought-wish" of each of them, etc. And now here they are, playing at couples and grown-ups and discounted baby clothes. Americo feels the tears welling in his eyes.

Anyway, the red wine is glorious. See how it swirls in the glass, so rich in body and color. Americo tastes it first; one sip, two, then downs the whole thing in one gulp. Mario regards him with a frozen-fish grin.

"Excuse me ...," Americo says, and flees to the bathroom.

He washes his face with cold water to see if it'll invigorate him. He can hear the distant voices of the women coming from the living room—"huge packages," "discount vouchers," "in that supermarket"—and wants only to scream and punch the baby-blue walls until his hands bleed. He shuts his eyes, tries to calm himself. It'll pass, it's all right, it'll be okay. Breathe deep, easy now.

The sound of the city, far off, beneath the hum of the fan in the bathroom ceiling. The muffled whooshing of automobiles, clothes swaying on the line. It must be beautiful outside.

Facing the mirror, eyes closed, Americo slips his hand in his pants and thinks of Carla Bruna. He sees her seated on the bed, naked from the waist up, smoking, as if she were alone. Her eyes almost woeful, she is turned toward the square of light from the window, concentrating on some terribly pragmatic idea. Americo thinks of her, of her head, of her dark nipples, of the contempt she can show towards him and towards life in general, and gradually ... suddenly ... gradually ... suddenly ... an intense sunlight streams through. Yes, suddenly the sun invades the Rodrigues' bathroom, a good and silent sun. So sudden and so peaceful and so good. Until someone knocks on the door.

"Is everything okay?" It's Joana. "Americo, are you all right?"

"Yes, thanks. It's just a … little intestinal complication, darling. I'll be right out."

He hears her steps going away (the fine black high-heeled shoes that cost three hundred and seventy-five euros, according to their credit card statement) and further off, from the living room, the cackles of The Nothing. He doesn't want to leave the bathroom. No, no, no. He won't leave here for anything on Earth.

There is a similar scene in *Being Paul Giamatti*. Americo, that is, the bogus Giamatti, is in the bathroom of a huge mansion in Los Angeles. It's one of those parties you see in the movies, with loud music, cocaine, naked people in the pool, that kind of shindig, and he's locked in the bathroom. The doorknob is shaped like a hand. Giamatti looks at it, somewhat distressed. He steels himself and tries to turn it. But the thing won't budge. It's not a doorknob, it's a hand. How odd. The macabre discovery sinks in slowly. A hand? But whose? The actor-character begins to feel queasy, starts sweating like a pig (close-up of massive drops of sweat running down his bald scalp), he is hyperventilating, there isn't enough air in such a closed, cramped, and sinister place.

Back at the party the houseguests laugh, cups in hand, showing their perfect teeth.

Giamatti pulls out a piece of paper from his pocket, unfolds it. *Three Steps To Control Your Panic Attacks*. He reads the first step, *Try to control your breathing*, and this is when he really starts to panic. His eyes ache from within, behind the eyeballs (close-up of wide eyes in expression of terror; cut to close-up on back of eyeballs, veins aflame, a chiaroscuro of night-black and green tints that recalls the bombing of Iraq), and he decides he has only one option: to scream. To scream as loudly as he can, to cry for help—HELP!—to see if anyone will come to his rescue, please.

But the music is way too loud; nobody hears a thing. *Oh God, I'm going to die here, what an idiotic way to go. No, it can't happen like this.* He screams more loudly. He cries and screams at once.

He desperately pounds the door with his fists, bangs it with his head.

From the other side, nothing. Only the happy *boom-boom* of the dance tunes.

He's on the floor drooling when Penélope Cruz opens the door. "May I, is this free?" asks the Spanish film star whose smile, upon seeing him in this condition, transforms into an expression of disgust and then to one of pity. As if he were a poor soul condemned to death.

Giamatti, pathetic puppy, exits on all fours. "Excuse me," she says and shuts the door.

Outside, he stands up, shakes his hands, thinks, *Suicide* (close-up of the word *Suicide* blinking on his imbecilic face), looks for the big kitchen in the big producer's big mansion, pulls a big whipped-cream cake out of the big refrigerator and devours it like a big rabid beast.

That night, back at the house, Joana asks him if he thinks Mariana has put on some weight.

"But she's pregnant, isn't she?"

"Even so ..."

"Yes," he says. "Maybe she has."

When his wife turns out the light, he doesn't close his eyes. He won't succumb so easily. He turns on his back, waits a moment to acclimate to the dark, and positions himself to gaze at those glowing things on the ceiling. Every night he sees them, every night they're different; he doesn't know how. Tonight they form a series of quickly flashing specks, appearing and disappearing. Little concise and comical circles that somehow resemble those people who have no idea how to move their bodies when they dance, how to produce a movement that could even be perceived as dance, but who nonetheless, what the fuck, try anyway.

4. Chocolate and Cookies

Americo puts aside, with an inexplicable sense of shame, *The Expletive* by Eduardo Fontes, a quite curious and clever book, completely worthy of the countless literary awards it has received abroad and, as the glowing reviews in Portugal's two major newspapers attest, an "indisputably ingenious work of great profundity and supreme linguistic invention" and a "highly efficient deconstruction of the artificial demarcation between the banal and the philosophical, the philosophical and the banal." This is all his fault, of course: he has neither the patience for "profundity" nor the head for "invention"; he just needs a few laughs. He plops the tome onto the shelf of postponed reads and grabs the first one off the next pile: *The Flower of Life* by Julio Abilio Pereirinha. This novel, from another renowned Portuguese author, received high praise from the very newspapers, magazines, and critics that so adored Fontes' work. *The Flower of Life*, they said, was "very, very good," "magnificent," "searing," "touched with genius," and "a must-read." Americo tries not to think too much about this and opens the book before Joachim awakens; otherwise he'll have no time to read any literature at all—good, bad, or indifferent.

There's a pretentious inscription on the first page, "I dedicate this book to all hearts of stone," and the first paragraph is a bit slow, stuffed with adverbs, but after that the story picks up some steam. A woman in a rolled-up skirt washes clothes in a tub on an "obscenely hot" day and, only two paragraphs later, a young girl reads "a classic of erotic French poetry" while hiding from the sanctimonious village shrews. What some people won't do to avoid a day's labor. Half an hour later Americo gives in himself. He shuts *The Flower of Life* and imagines his Falstaff, his project for a refined and demanding yet lighthearted theater that will reach the common folk.

The lights come up. Falstaff is dressed as a firefighter. On the back of his uniform, "Falstaff" is written, just like on a football jersey, and below that: "Volunteer Fireman." He's a fat man (pillows under his clothes) with a fake red nose (it looks like a potato). He enters the firehouse, sits down on the first chair he sees. He adopts the attitude of someone who's been there a long time and is sick and tired of waiting.

Americo can relate. He, too, is sick and tired of waiting around and doing nothing. He lies down on the couch, closes his eyes. He has a fiercely strange dream.

He is sitting at a table in a restaurant, waiting. The other tables—dozens, hundreds of them, all square and covered with white tablecloths—are empty; there's not a waiter in sight. And yet he senses that he is being spied on, perhaps by one of those surveillance cameras hidden behind smoked glass. He plays it cool, looks around. It's an old and ample room. A huge chandelier dangles in the middle like some notion out of the past. Suddenly, from a darkened space he hadn't yet noticed, a red curtain opens and a group of women masquerading as mothers (baggy dresses, breast pumps fastened to their chests) begin dancing a hybrid, a clumsy cancan mixed with a botched burlesque or who knows what. When they make a full turn, Americo notices some cylinders (like diver's tanks but made of transparent glass) attached to their backs, filled with a white, semi-viscous liquid that may or may not be milk. He is far away, seated at a remove from them in his own corner, facing an empty plate, and he has the sensation that they are unaware of his presence. Suddenly, an arm appears and puts a glass of tomato juice on his table. When he turns, the waiter has already vanished. Americo wants to tell him that he hasn't ordered anything, that there's been some mistake, but the man doesn't return. The chandelier sways imperceptibly in the middle of the room.

Americo raises the glass to his lips. A familiar flavor, he knows it well. Neither tomato nor milk. He looks toward the women and feels adult, sated. The two words appear to him in the dream: *adult, sated.* How great that he can come to a restaurant by himself, free, the master of his own time. Conscious of the significance of this luxury, he leans back on his chair, smiling. He is content, arms resting on the white tablecloth (now incandescent), savoring everything around him—the dance routine of the mock mothers, the cancan of the milk-squirting breasts—and it is at this moment it comes to him: Blood. It's blood he's been drinking. My God, blood. He puts down the glass and stands up to leave. "This is unacceptable .... You have no right!"

The dance stops, the women all look at him. They are naked now and very beautiful. Yet it is not desire that Americo feels. On the contrary: there is now, on the faces of the women, a deep, prosaic melancholy, a puniness, an expression of boundless evil. He hears a terrible scream.

Americo runs away in a panic and, impossibly, traverses the wall into the street.

Hundreds of orange buses whizz past him. He's on the outskirts of town, on foot, on a highway he doesn't recognize. Pieces of metal lie strewn along the shoulder. A few meters ahead, a double-decker bus is turned upside-down, cut in half. A human body, neither male nor female, hangs from some twisted shards of iron. All is quiet. Americo doesn't want to look, yet he is compelled to look, when his son awakens, screaming.

"Coming ..."

The kid doesn't stop.

"Christ, I'm coming already!"

Joachim keeps yelling and Americo gets up. In an attempt to calm him down, he carries the boy into the living room, sits him on his lap and turns the television on to the soccer channel. Lichtenstein is playing Malta. A friendly, in preparation for a World Cup qualifier. It ends in a scoreless tie, ninety-four minutes later.

Joana arrives late in the afternoon, exhausted but babbling on endlessly about topics that, later, Americo will do his best to forget, circular monologues about "the surreal issues that we face concerning the implementation of a plan to regulate the quality of olive oil in this country." After managing (with great difficulty) to put Joachim to bed, they dine on some frozen, precooked things: meatballs and a mysterious green cube described on the package as "vegetable concentrate." They watch a game show on TV, after which Joana spends about half an hour on the computer, doing some work, while Americo puts the dirty dishes in the dishwasher.

This is the chore he hates more than any on Earth. Handling those plates, caked with mashed potatoes and gravy, with scraps of meat or fish or vegetables, with tiny bites of unrecognizable organic matter, the remains of meat or fish or vegetables that look like they've been chewed up and vomited on to the plate in tiny pieces, to tolerate the stench, all those horrid odors mixed up with his own in that stuffy kitchen, all of it reminds him only of disease and dissipation and death. Yes, dirty dishes upset him profoundly. The scraps of food on the piled-up plates always make him think of his sick and crippled father in the Happy Rest nursing home over in Sintra.

If you travel on IC-19 you can see the huge billboard on the right showing two smiling seniors and the words *Happy Rest* as though written by hand (a giant hand, capable of crushing an automobile), then you turn off at the next exit, go around the traffic circle, follow the sign that reads *Health Unit* and there you are; fifty meters farther and you arrive at the gate. Americo's father is the white-haired man seated next to the table where they play gin rummy and spades.

He's been in a wheelchair for four years now. One Wednesday he suffered an accident while carrying home a TV set. A brand-new plasma flat-screen Hayku-Flash 3.0 with two remotes included. He slipped on the steps in the shopping mall on his way to the car park elevator. It didn't seem very serious at first, but after a while it left him unable to move, and finally he began to experience "personality shifts." He would shout random insults at perfect strangers, laugh and cry unprompted, and, with his eyes fixed on some irrelevant detail—a stain on the wall, a fly, some dust on St. Anthony's head in the living room—spend hours without saying a word. He had once been a professor of cultural anthropology, which is probably why his preferred epithet, in the months following the accident, was "Fucking pygmies!" He employed the insult indiscriminately, spraying everyone in range with it everywhere, as if the world were to blame for his condition. It was a huge relief for everyone when Americo's mother divorced him and the family brought him to the Happy Rest. Anyway, these are the kinds of things that leave their marks.

Every now and then, when Americo is distracted by some soccer commentary on the car radio, passing by signs with funny place names like *Chunkville* or *Girl Market* or *Tubetown*, or reading the gigantic letters advertising mini golf—*boom!*—he'll suddenly think of his father. It's kind of a nice sensation, as if someone were stapling his brain with soft little stitches. It doesn't hurt so much once you get used to it. But little by little it wears on him, scrapes at old scabs, snatches tiny bits of his soul. Yes, all this stuff comes to him whenever he sticks dirty plates in the dishwasher. His poor old Dad. The last time he pays him a visit, he doesn't even recognize him, or pretends not to.

"So, Dad, how's it going? Cheating at cards again?"

His father lifts his eyes from the cards, looks at him shamelessly. The serious look of a madman. It puts a scare into him, but Americo uses his actor training not to reveal his feelings. It's something he's never before seen on his father's face: a glazed look of sheer terror. And what if his father flies into a capricious rage and attacks him? A grisly scene involving nails and teeth, or skin and blood? Or surgical blows against the head and chest, hitting all the pressure points? Were his hands always this hairy?

But his father only smiles. "Professor Orestes, long time no see!"

Americo tries to smile, too. A young nurse with a long face, having seen enough, and mortified for him, diverts her eyes.

His father crosses his arms. "Time hasn't passed for you, Professor Orestes!"

Americo gasps. "I …." Should he tell him that this is Americo, his son, his one and only son? Or not? Under the pressure of the moment, a swelling silence fills the room; he feels each moment like a violence, a pinprick to the middle of his forehead just above the eyes, a needle to his skull that reaches straight through to his thoughts, and he takes the easy way out. He half-turns and smiles a yellow smile.

When he is back home in bed, Joana asks him if everything is all right. Americo says yes. He undresses slowly, puts on the striped pajamas the maid left folded beneath the pillow. She's a tall Moldavian woman, the maid, nice enough but a little intimidating. Her name is Ada. Is that how it's written, he wonders, like a palindrome? Lying down now, the sheets pulled up to his chin, he tries to conjure a little diversion from that afternoon.

Ada as a nymphomaniacal nurse. (It's nothing, really, just something to pass the time before nodding off.) He is a kind of wounded war hero lying in a hospital bed pretending to sleep but is actually quite alert and focused, listening to her approach. The sound of high heels on the hypothetical floor. Americo feels a burgeoning contentment, the anticipation builds, the imagining, Ada, Ada. But none of this diminishes the fright he gets when her voice whispers in his ear, "Come." He pivots to embrace her, but the hallucination has already passed; he's suddenly aware that he's not with the masquerading Ada, of course, but with his wife Joana, who wants to fulfill her day by showing him how much she loves him and how happy they are; how normal and pretty is this picture- postcard of bliss they live within.

While they thrash about, and she whispers in his ear some monotonous spiel about "visualizing him" visiting her years from now in her workplace and fucking her in the Subdirector's office while her colleagues and supervisors on the either side of the wall stamp reports and papers and other stupid official documents with no clue as to what's going on, he keeps his eyes open and locked on the wall. He repeats yes, yes, oh yes, to her slack little fantasy and fixes his gaze at a black line on the white wall, a trivial detail—just like his father, altered after the tumble, his happy, paralyzed, mad father—he gazes at the dark wound and thinks of air pumps. Intricate, dirty, noisy machines with cogwheels and pistons churning up and down, up and down in a monotonous air-pumping fury. Just then she lets go a shriek and he lets himself go—*ahh*. It's all over.

"My love," she says.

"My darling," he says.

But he's not sleepy. He waits, counts silently to a hundred. He waits a little longer. Joana's breathing shifts; it's slower, more rhythmic. She's asleep for sure.

Americo gets out of bed, puts on his slippers, slides wistfully to the kitchen. He opens the pantry and pulls out the boxes of rice, the packages of pasta, the cans of beans, tomatoes, chickpeas, tuna. He fumbles around in the depths of the cabinet, finds nothing. Nothing. He finished the chocolate? How can that be? Not a morsel remains of that chocolate bar he kept stashed there for emergencies like this one. My God, not even a puny little square? He feels a horrible emptiness. He has to eat something to quiet this nameless malaise, something that will directly gratify the pleasure center in his brain, but what, goddammit, what?

Once, when he was a little kid, in a vacation house that his parents had rented in the Algarve, he awoke in the middle of the night and forced himself to walk to the room at the end of the corridor. With an inchoate need to experience terror, he opened the door slowly and stepped inside. There was no one there, just a roomful of air. He took two steps, stopped. His heart beat rapidly; his hands sweated. He felt a weird vertigo, a compression, as if a helmet of air he wore on his head had suddenly transformed into stone. But he didn't budge. All part of the game. He stood there, unmoving, speechless, for ten long seconds in the dark.

Mixed with this desire to scare himself shitless was the hazy notion to tell it all later to his dad, so that he would know how brave and grown-up his son was. But in the end he told no one. He kept it all to himself, perhaps out of pride, who knows. Or maybe it was just that the next morning he let the opportunity pass and later it didn't seem possible to recount. How pathetic it is telling this story—so brittle, so intimate—now that time has changed everything.

In the kitchen now, in the middle of the night, he feels utterly lost. He needs some comfort food—something sugary, something sweet—to restore his equilibrium and put a stop to these inner tremors. This is not fear he's feeling, nothing like it. Just a little psychological vertigo. He opens the cookie tin and—oh shit, empty. Dear God, totally empty. He was sure there were some left, the ones with the chocolate chips, from that package he bought last week. Three or four cookies at the very least. Mother of God, nothing? Americo clutches the round tin—the size of a birthday cake—red on the outside, metallic on the inside—and feels the air stiffening against his eyes and his chest. He turns the key in the kitchen door, sits down on a wobbly chair and remembers when he was little and could summon the fear of vacant rooms. *Saudade*, that's the word for it. How shameless, a grown man with such namby-pamby notions.

When he gets back to the bedroom he receives quite a fright.

"What happened?" Joana screams.

"Nothing, honey. It's all good .... I just had to pee."

Joana asks no more questions and he, too, remains silent. For half a minute he stands motionless in the dark, then climbs into bed. He sucks in a breath, looks at her face. She seems to have fallen back to sleep. Or maybe she hadn't fully awoken and had shouted the words from deep in some dream. Maybe she is dreaming that she is asleep and that someone has crawled into her bed. Yeah, *her* bed. Which is exactly what Americo hates about this house. Everything is hers, the bed, everything, all this useless junk and none of it actually his.

Tonight there are no little lights blinking in the ceiling.

He turns away from his wife and closes his eyes. Now it's serious, now he will sleep, in total silence. As the Deaf Man says in the final scene of the *Chronicle of Pure Rhetoric*, the notorious farce attributed to a master scribe in the court of Dom Sebastian I, "Oh Silence, if you weren't such a chatterbox, the things of this world would more truly speak of its mysteries ...." Fuck, what he wouldn't give for just one of those chocolates made with 70 percent real cocoa powder.

5. *Theater of War*, Now That's a Great Title

"But didn't it all come to nothing?" asks Murilo, who seems more disheveled and spaced out every day.

Americo looks at him, expressionless, as if he hadn't understood the question. "No," he says bluntly. "It's definitely legit. The thing's gonna happen."

"Well, congratulations. You know, it was a helluva lucky thing. The Englishman happened to call me during the only twenty-five minutes I spent in the office that day."

"For sure. And those guys pay like nobody's business."

"I wonder who told him that I knew you."

"Yeah, man, soon I'll learn how to do things, Hollywood style."

"What … are you going to America, Americo?"

"Ha ha. Nah, it'll be shot here. My part, anyway. Somewhere outside of Lisbon, in the provinces. A site called Place of the Inner Arches, heard of it? Anyway, the location's near there. In Trás-Os-Montes, I think …"

"Never heard of it."

"Or over by Alto Douro somewhere … me neither."

They drink beers in Café Viseense and watch the people pass by the other side of the window. On the street, amidst the abandoned bottles of port in the shop window, folks with their heads cut from view scurry to important appointments. "But for the time being, the shoot's on hold."

"Welcome to Portugal, my son."

"Actually, it was a screwup on their end. A change of screenwriter, a ' pre-production alteration to the script.'"

"I see."

"And I'm going to act with Penélope Cruz."

"No way!"

"Pe-né-lo-pe."

"You're kidding me."

"Oh yeah. It's all in writing, in black-and-white. Unless this script alteration ..."

"And does Joana know?"

"Yeah ... I think so."

"You haven't even told her."

"Damn, I just hope they don't change that part of it."

"Amen to that," Murilo sighs.

On the other side of the window, the headless people of Lisbon slide past, gorged with sun and reflected light. Watching them, Americo is seized with an immense fatigue. He's been here before, seated in this exact chair. Back arched, beer in hand, he gazes at the parade of faceless, workaday phantoms. A morbid tedium ensues. "Hey, waiter ..."

The waiter turns around. "Yes?" he says looking not at him, but at his forehead.

Americo doesn't know what to say; he just stands there.

"Well, what can I do for you?" the man asks, with the petrified look of someone staring at the relic of St. Teotonio's arm in the Viseu Cathedral.

"One more," Americo responds, indicating his empty glass. He doesn't add a "please" or anything else, and diverts his eyes before finishing the sentence. He too knows how to be nasty. A wretched, guilt-ridden prick.

The waiter goes off to fetch the beer and Americo chuckles to himself. Don't look at the customer, don't expect a "please." There's your lesson for today. And, what a relief it is, just to feel anything. Sometimes it's good to be wicked. Suddenly he feels almost fine.

Next to him Murilo is talking about a mutual friend, someone he knows better than Americo, a guy named Areyas, who is separated from his wife (one fine day he spotted her sitting on the lap of a stranger in an orange shirt in the playground of a service area off the Porto-Braga highway), a guy who has had some savage incidents in two or three Lisbon bars, before leaving for some alleged holidays in Europe, a trajectory that supposedly included Spain, France, and Italy, as well as Luxembourg and Albania, and has now returned, filled with megalomaniacal notions and on the verge of nervous collapse. Murilo says that he is much leaner and that his eyes have gotten bigger and bluer—"You think that's possible?"—he suspects the poor schmuck has taken to writing poetry and that by now he must be completely broke. Speaking of money, Murilo recalls when he and Areyas, back when they were both around twelve or thirteen, concocted a scheme to rob the Bank of Portugal, where Murilo's father worked as a "cadre clerk." (A term, he says, that for many years sounded top secret to him, as if "cadre" were some kind of security area, an invisible but actual territory within the thick walls of the bank, a "state" unto itself, with its own signs, language, and laws, and with a different and denser oxygen.) The plan consisted of a series of A5 sheets of paper covered with schemes and calculations, blueprints and arrows, question marks, drawings, caricatures, newspaper clippings, etc., but the whole idea boiled down to stealing Mr. Areyas' trench coat and removing his car keys, after which both of them would enter the Bank of Portugal disguised as Mr. Areyas (piggyback inside his coat, one of top of the other, like in a comic strip), seduce Dona Liliana, Mr. Areyas' secretary who young Areyas had once seen at a party and who, he swore, was just as hot a babe as Brigitte Bardot, breach the main vault using the master key they got off the "generous" secretary, and finally, digging a tunnel to the Tejo River and escaping in a motorboat. "Stealing away to sea like in the movies," Murilo adds, and Americo can't help but feel that behind all of this grandiose nostalgia lurks the gloom of a much darker malevolence than his own, a pleasure in recounting the protracted details of other people's downfalls. As if Areyas were already dead and buried and Murilo derived a twisted gratification from it.

"He was the talented kind, full of potential ...," says Murilo, as he ogles the waitress scrubbing cups in the sink.

Americo imagines him some day in the future telling someone similar things about himself. How amusing he once was, how brilliant as a young man, how he was, he was, he was, and no longer is, washed up before his time. But he says nothing.

"There was that song, 'Areias Is a Camel.'"

The conversation shifts to the tax hikes, the sorry state of politics, soccer's decline into a circus, and winds up at disease: friends or acquaintances stricken overnight with Alzheimer's, Parkinson's, pneumonia, schizophrenia, brain or heart trouble, depression, cancer, just like that.

"Look at that," Murilo says. "The way her hips shimmy when she scrubs."

"Shh ... keep your voice down."

They part in the street, beneath a barbaric sun. They shake hands while still talking and suggest meeting up again the following week. Just before turning his back, Murilo flashes that lyrical old smile of his. He's off to meet a woman, for sure. Who will it be this time? Another neurotic young intern? Another crazy, divorced cougar-colleague? Another shopgirl, another optician? And why hasn't he provided any details?

When he gets home, Americo's scalp is on fire. He sticks his head under the faucet. Cold water! First he shrieks, then he laughs. He looks at himself in the mirror, amused. *Tres* Giamatti.

His hair still dripping, he sits at his desk. Come on now, relax, focus. He's free, must make full use of every minute. Today Joachim is staying at his grandmother's, destroying her tchotchkes and rehearsing new screaming techniques. Before commencing, the actor snaps his fingers like a cut-rate pianist. He breathes deeply, opens a new document on the computer, and writes on the blank screen: *Title?* Today, for certain, he'll get some real work done. Today is the day.

He gazes at the white in the screen. It's a false, dull white void. Not a single word. And his belly is making noises. Could it be from those few sips of beer? To erase any doubts, he goes into the kitchen to have another little lunch. Café au lait and bread with guava jelly, two sandwiches' worth, oh yeah.

The Falstaff project is going nowhere, that's for sure. Joana is right about that. Shakespeare and volunteer firemen ... it's missing something, some hook, something to spice it up, to give it some oomph, some originality. But if not Falstaff, then what? In the kitchen Americo looks at a rotten apple in the fruit basket, a brown circle in a red sphere.

Some Brecht, perhaps? Considering that much of the culture crowd was weaned on the German theater, the time when it seemed it might become a real force for world change. "Brecht," says Americo, in the empty kitchen, trying to get the pronunciation down just right. Stress on the "r" and the "t": "Bertolt Brecht." The name itself can effect miracles; the mere sound of it will open doors, a magic word uttered in the right office could get even the biggest theatre bigwig to pick up his cell phone. Drop the word "Brecht" on their voicemail, and *boom!*—you're in, danke verrry much! It could be one of his lesser known, more didactic plays, wordy and politically incorrect, one of his "unperformable" ones, an avant-garde rendition, deconstructed like crazy.

Looking right through the apple, Americo envisions actors in blackface wearing kinky wigs and others made up with yellow skin and Asian eyes. A team of workmen played only by women, and everyone else, men and women, played by women. It might even be interesting to conflate the revolutionary rhetoric with something Grecian, something in the vein of *The Bacchae*. Stir in some intelligent sex. But then again ... maybe not. The *das politik* approach has seen better days. It's pretty clear that most people—promoters, journalists, the general public—no longer take to these things with the same innocence and exuberance as they once did. They hide themselves behind inscrutable, meaningless smiles, applaud in rhythmic, restrained ovations that barely last through the second curtain call. By the end of this encore, when the cast has yet to leave the stage, and you can already sense the silence setting in, the pain sears into the cultured heart. No, definitely nothing political, bad idea, won't sell. Forget Brecht. How about Beckett?

A Beckett taken to the limit, a Beckett beyond Beckett, so *Beckettian* that no one in this ultrapoetic country has ever imagined it. An infinite landscape—a denuded landscape, infinitely white, cold as metal—with actors that are there and not there, actors who are nothing but mouths and hats, shoes and lapels, dirty, skinny legs, utterly sexless cleavage. Americo can see it all quite clearly: the dark stage, lights trained on each detail, on each close-up; actors composed of only their parts, gradually coming together, emerging from voice and from speech, people comprised of image and text. Heads, torsos, severed phrases. Enacting, that is, the actual detachment they feel. Yes, that's it. A Pessoan Beckett, and thus, the most Beckettian of all. And one, therefore, more our own. On the other hand ... well, is there any Beckett we haven't seen around here thousands of times already?

Americo gets up and opens the window. What about a superclassic Portuguese play tailored to today's times? A "brash reinterpretation," an "audacious revival"? A sort of post-modern Gil Vicente, in which Hell isn't quite so bad, Heaven's a bit of a bore, and Purgatory is a normal, nine-to-five work week, just like real life? A Gil Vicente set in traffic, at a customer-service counter, in a hospital elevator? Or a contemporary text, Nordic, perhaps, or German or English,

Irish, Scottish, Gaelic? A circus comedy? A poetry reading? A word-less drama? A musical?

Back at his computer, Americo highlights the paragraph about Falstaff as a volunteer fireman, presses the key and—*zap!*—it vanishes. Theater, forget it. And then, for no apparent reason (or because he has just eaten bread with guava jelly, something he hasn't eaten in years, not since the time of this particular memory, when he was sixteen or seventeen), it strikes him: the day he spent in a poor neighborhood on the outskirts of Lisbon, an area called L or M or S (like a size marker on a clothing tag). He was with Murilo and Manel, a friend from those days, a very tall and thin dude with a penchant for cardigans who some people called, for some reason, The Atrium. The three of them went to help out in a community center run by a friend of Manel, a girl that studied psychology and, as a committed Catholic, spent her spare time doing volunteer work. The Atrium had a little crush on her, and even though she didn't reciprocate, he would do anything she asked, and Americo and Murilo would tag along, just to help out, because the girl was actually quite ingratiating; also they weren't totally against the idea of saving the world and conquering injustice and, in the end, they had nothing better to do. The community center was in a really bad neighborhood. There were no junkies in sight, like those images you sometimes see in the news, but there were shacks made of brick and tin with exposed concrete and holes for windows. Americo also vaguely remembers some spongy materials, dark fabrics or blue tarps covering certain parts of the houses, which gave the impression that tiny pieces of sky had fallen and melted over the living rooms and bedrooms and bathrooms of these folks. But then again this could all be an exaggeration; perhaps it's an image that only came to him later, in long-forgotten nightmares later morphed into actual memories. And these kinds of neighborhoods still exist, there and elsewhere, as do those people, or others like them, or their sons and daughters, whatever, they continue to live this way, gouging out bricks just to get some light, burying their heads in pillows at night so as not to hear the creatures scurrying in the walls, so as not to smell the open sewer, so as not to imagine a life beyond this one, another place where there are real windows and the sky doesn't fall. And with all of this, what can theater possibly offer? What can theater—Christ, what a joke— possibly do? To expose—expose? Shit, that's its big fucking response? But what can it offer if no one, or almost no one, goes to the theater, and those who do go couldn't care less? What can it offer if theater no longer has the power to ignite a fire in the bosom of society (what a marvelous expression that is, "the bosom of society"), if today it has become dismal and dull and trapped in the snare of believing what others say about it, of what is imposed upon it from afar with a kind of benign neglect so that nowadays it can be only two things, two variants on mutually exclusive failure: either the "opiate of the mass- es" or "bourgeois dilettantism"? No, if the theater could once spark ideas and bring about change, it no longer can. Give it up, guillotine this notion of theater once and for all. Politics, that's the thing. Poli- tics! Politics! Politics is back! Power: the real power is in persuading the guilty to plant potatoes, to get the monkeys to walk the plank, to, well, whatever the expression is. The power to oblige the haves to give to the have-nots, the power to spawn a new society, to offer everyone a fresh start, the rich who've lost their joy, the poor who've lost their future, the middle class who've lost their dreams, an entire populace condemned to repeat, tirelessly, the slogans of the cabbies and the tabloids: "They're all the same, they're all crooks, yada yada yada." Politics: only through the panoramic prism of politics can the slums of S or L or XL be eradicated, these neighborhoods that arrest our hearts in perpetual adolescence, consuming us with a guilt that isn't ours but from which no bleach or rationalization or entertain- ment on Earth can cleanse us. In the end, it's the burden of original sin that we lug around these days. A divided, unjust, and dreadful world in which some possess sumptuous mansions with swimming pools—the whole living sky—and others only tiny pieces of that sky to cover the holes in the roofs of their shacks and a bucket in the corner to catch the rain.

Exuberant, moved almost to tears, Americo imagines himself—with the body he has now but with the chubbier face of his adolescence—charging into politics full of ideals and lofty hopes. In a suit and tie, of course, like all serious politicians (those on the far left who refuse to wear conventional attire are, deep down, really just a bunch of marketers, as if showing up in shirtsleeves or worse, in a turtleneck, were proof of being "outside the system," as if this alone could make them seem more serious in our eyes, more dignified, more "like us," hell, when actually this only reveals what bloody snobs they are, that is to say the opposite kind, reverse snobs, which may make it even more insulting, yes, yes, that is, no, he sees himself in a suit and tie, of course), but a modest one like those worn by bank clerks or the freshly-graduated, not those Italian extravagances but a cheap ready-to-wear ensemble, accentuated by a sober tie with a faint touch of originality and some black-rimmed retro-futurist glasses. Yes, some farsighted glasses, so it won't take too long to recognize those who break from the mob, the great mob that, in this reverie, owns every single voter in continental Portugal, the archipelagos of Madeira and the Azores and the Entire Community of Expatriates scattered across the four corners of the globe—people emerging from the mass of *numbers-statistics-polls* with their hands outstretched, anonymous people transforming into names and faces and eyes and mouths that motivate and exhort him to press on, to proceed with hope, fueling him with positive energy for the arduous path ahead. Americo rises, goes to the balcony to look out over the city. He sees himself atop a flatbed truck speaking to attentive crowds. He imagines himself on television debating with the other candidates under intense bright lights. He sees himself inside office spaces with brown or beige walls signing documents, taking phone calls, compromising, saying yes to imbeciles, accepting what he judges as simply the "rules of the game" but ultimately reveals itself to be an accelerating and premature old age, a chilling detachment, cynicism, envy and betrayal, realizing in the end that the transformation he once believed in so ardently will take way too long, an eternity to accomplish, so long, in fact, that it will never happen, realizing finally that words are hollow, that the world is a much more difficult place than he once supposed and recoils against itself like a great rubber band, always on the verge of snapping, realizing that inertia is a poison, that lies are a poison, and that this poison has gotten inside him—it's in his body, the muscles of his face when he speaks, realizing that he is turning into something else, a lesser, lazier creature, a stick figure, a clone of himself—realizing that, little by little, without anyone noticing, he has transformed into something inert and slipshod, something of banal grandeur, something akin to—is this possible?—an armchair. Ladies and gentlemen, boys and girls, here is our great political leader, the incredible, unprecedented …Armchair Man! The goings-on outside the windows are now at the mercy of his remote control. Just push a button and voilà! The sheer power of it. The great leader, the Armchair, settles into himself, true, but it's such a good and comfortable sensation that he never wants to be free of it. He continues in this fashion, without altering a single comma, keeps going, lets himself go, randomly flashes his false yellow smile to everyone, to his left and to his right. As if he were a walking photo op. As if heaven were the same as hell and everything that has been will be and nothing has ever changed and nothing ever will, amen. Only by force, by the force of his own hands. Only by laying his head on the chopping block and exposing his throat to the blade of the guillotine. Only by having the guts to start a revolution. Yes, the "revolution." Americo is not afraid to say it aloud, to shout the bloody word to the rafters. Yes, only by force, by arms, taking everything by storm. Shatter political compromises, click off the country, the world, then click it on again, channel by channel, a whole new season. But doesn't that imply violence? At least a little bit of violence? Wouldn't that involve, wouldn't it have to involve, just a little, just a touch, just an itsy-bitsy

teenie-weenie amount of blood and crying mothers and teenage sol-
diers with the better part of their brains blown out and honest and
respectable folks plagued by evil armies and rapists and pillagers and
the bloodthirsty and arsonists running wild and torched villages and
buildings in rubble and charred landscapes and defenseless children
left in remote houses in the middle of the mountains, in the middle
of the night, naked nursery school children abandoned on dark
wooden tables crying and screaming and waving their little arms in
the void, in the silence, in the unfeeling and senseless emptiness. And
can he imagine himself in camouflage, smelling of sweat and food
scraps, thinner and fitter than he is now, with bigger eyes, protruding
from their sockets, the eyes of a saint or a zealot, more translucent
than ever, crawling around, holes in the elbows of his sleeves, knees
transformed into giant calluses, his hair thicker and sprouting in new
places, on his shoulders and above his ears, a machine gun strapped
to his back, advancing slowly but purposefully, trying to maintain
the pace without losing faith, wriggling his way silently, as silently as
possible, atop dirt and pine needles and sticks and stones, his mouth
shut, breathing through his nose to stave off a sore throat in such a
hostile environment, sensing the presence of creatures, above and
below him, crawling around like a beast himself, toward the secret
bunker that he knows as "headquarters," a cave, a hollow pit somewhere in Monsanto, in the Leiria Pines, in a lost slope behind the
Starry Mountains, a cold, dank, confining hole, where he keeps his
meager belongings, a sleeping bag and a laptop, a few cans of tuna,
immense sheets of paper (folded in odd and endearing ways, like
burial flags), where he studies blueprints of army barracks, squad-
rons, government and other public buildings of "strategic impor-
tance," attempting to commit them to memory; an instruction man-
ual on "homemade explosives" he downloaded off the Internet, a
theoretical tome with the title *Revolution and Guerilla Warfare*, a
ruled notebook that functions as his diary, a No. 2 pencil, a No. 3
pencil, a Bic ballpoint pen, toilet paper, aspirin, a pair of scissors, nail

clippers, rubbing alcohol—can he imagine himself like this? As a revolutionary, without soap or toothpaste? Or even dental floss? Can he picture himself with this chiseled physique, obeying the rules of the battle-tested primer, following to the letter what is prescribed out of something called *How To Make History In Ten Easy Lessons*? Isn't that ridiculous? It's beyond ridiculous, even for him, an actor who can certainly appreciate a little farce. Christ, no, it's way too ridiculous, even compensating for the whole world changing once and forever. Yes, ridiculous. But what might be great would be a play about all this. But of course! A play, with a monologue laden with profundity, very contemporary, and sprinkled with hefty doses of humor. And what shall we call it? A technical term, something provocative or quasi-sentimental, a scholarly allusion, a catchphrase that stays with you without drawing your attention to it, a clear and simple title that suggests to the prospective audience the promise of a future classic. How about, for example, "Theater of War"? "Theater of War," now that's a great title. The sophisticated epic of a modern-day guerrilla-hero. The last true believer, a great visionary, the first actor of the legitimate theater to wield a machine gun. And is it "actor" or "actress"? A woman? But of course! My God, that's it, it has to be a woman, that gives it so much more credibility. At once unconventional and progressive. Women will soon be in charge, they're getting closer and closer, isn't that what they keep saying on all those high-minded morning radio shows? A woman, what a resoundingly inspired notion. Americo pictures a redhead, that magnificent, monumental, American redhead, the one who plays the executive secretary in that television series about the advertising world of 1950's New York, a grown woman with a girlish manner, the innocent-not-so-innocent type, spicy-hot, that delightful, truly voluptuous redhead, diabolically talented with a figure beyond classic, beyond modern, a la Mae West (whose body, according to historians, was the archetype for the first Coca-Cola bottle). Picture her dressed as a soldier, a guerrilla, an Amazon, wearing an outfit just snug enough to accommodate her movements, lying prone on a dark wooden stage. Surrounded by darkness with a spotlight trained on her, she crawls in the mud while looking ahead of her, at the people in the audience—are they allies or enemies?—all while narrating the story, what is happening, and how, and when, and within that account, a discourse that begins simply but gradually becomes dense and full of twists and turns; in the sacred manifestation of words the soldier-woman invents a parallel language to the Portuguese (though several times more oblique) in which she recounts her life, conflating world events with her own fantasies, deftly confusing eras in order to draw us more deeply into the story, opening and closing her thick lips in search of phrases that will project properly throughout the theater, gyrating her bright, bountiful eyes in search of the proper emotional effect upon the public (a faceless and shapeless mass, a totality without border or center, a dark blotch of collective breathing). Yes, this divine American on our very stage, stretching her thighs, lifting her neck, heaving her bosom, gyrating her butt, communicating, in essence, with her entire body, all of it, that body that unnerves him so much, in such a way that—Americo can't stand it anymore. Where is the cell phone? Where did he leave his fucking cell phone? He must call her; he's got to have her. He knows he shouldn't, that it's stupid and dangerous, but he has no choice. Today, girl, it'll be the opposite. Today he'll be the one who asks. Pressing the send button, there goes the text. He must find out if she likes him for *him*, if it's true that he's not just one of many, that he really, actually exists, that he's flesh and blood, that he's truly in her life. Carla Bruna, my brave, beastly, beautiful love.

6. This

Two days later, Americo stops at the newsstand to look at the headlines and reads this: "Luxury Escort Stabbed To Death. Bloody Violence In The Lisbon Night." Beneath the yellow letters, slightly askew, against a black background, Carla Bruna, with a look of astonishment on her face.

Americo bends over to vomit, but only dry-heaves. He feels faint, stricken by a sudden, deadly nausea, as if the news had imploded inside him, deep down in his belly, in his guts, and the shrapnel now spewed from his mouth. The taste of decay, of dust. He lifts up his eyes, reads the headline one more time. It's her, there's no doubt about it. It's an old photograph; she's a little younger, her skin a little paler, with wide eyes and a plunging neckline that this rag of a newspaper thought appropriate for the occasion. Can this really be his Carla Bruna?

"*The Scandal*, please …," he says, coins held in his trembling hand.

"So, it's a *Scandal* today, is it?" asks old Lopes, as if to shame him.

The wretched little man hands him the paper, and Americo flees in a dead run. He stumbles down the street filled with happy, placated city folk, for whom this is a day like any other—these content, clueless, detestable urbanites, these frighteningly normal types whom no tragedy has ever befallen—takes the corner by the building under construction, and stops. His heart pounding, he inhales deeply and, afraid of what comes next, opens *The Scandal*. A girl walking up the street looks at him as though there's a hole in his head. Americo turns toward the wall, and begins reading.

That night, at dinner at the home of his in-laws on the occasion of their thirty-fifth anniversary, he forces himself to appear easygoing and convivial. He laughs at old stories he's heard dozens of times, raves about the duck fried rice, the wine, the cake, the new tablecloth with the giant flowers stitched into the corners, and even contains himself—teeth clenched, good little boy—when his wife's father, Vicentino Rosas, launches into one of his habitual rants about the "the blacks, the browns, and the yellows," the whole lot of them a bunch of lazy, left-leaning riff-raff, blah-blah-blah. Dona Celeste presides over the meal with her customary sphinxlike demeanor, her eyes half-closed. None of this is intentional, it's just how she is. Whenever she catches the eye of one of the guests (there are eight of them: Americo's in-laws, Joana and himself, a cousin on Vincentino Rosas's side named Arthur, his wife—Marilia? Marianita?—and another couple in their sixties, the Mendes Fernandes, who are friends of the hosts), a taut, ear-to-ear smile appears on her face. In that brief moment she is the very image of benevolence and charity and love for others. The smile vanishes almost instantly. It doesn't fade gradually, like a normal smile, but collapses all at once. As if it were programmed to self-destruct the second it appears. A robo-smile.

"You don't like the wine?" Joana asks him. These days it's so rare to see her this way, so animated, so jubilant.

"It's ... excellent."

She's older now, of course, but still strikingly, objectively beautiful, as indisputably stunning a babe as when they first met, at a wedding reception more than ten years ago. Christ, how long ago that was! And those newlyweds, Anabela Reis and Armando Ruas—what characters!—now divorced. She hit him on the head with an electric guitar and he ran off with those twin bimbos in a rented Jeep. Twirling her wedding ring around on her finger (only now does Americo notice that her nails are painted a shocking pink), Joana mentions that she ran into a friend, graduated from a good university with a political science degree, working in a shoe store at the shopping mall. Mendes Fernandes, who teaches in Coimbra, says that a university degree means nothing today. Vicentino Rosas sighs and shakes his head, as if to say, "How tragic, what a waste," and does it with such conviction, with such authentic melancholy, that the topic dies right then and there and everyone forgets the story of Joana's unfortunate friend.

A little later, Mrs. Mendes Fernandes, who is not a professor but who has worked for a horrendous number of years at the National Institute for the Prevention of Highway Accidents, reveals that the wine's particular combination of varietals makes it one of a kind the world over. Everyone registers their surprise and satisfaction at this and wine becomes the next big topic at the table. Reds versus whites, the improving rosés, good and bad years, Portuguese and foreign vintages, Old World and New World, young wines versus old, single varietals, winemakers, casks, wine critics, etc. Suddenly, like someone who remembers a pot burning on the stove, Dona Celeste turns her head, "Isn't it much too cold?"

"The wine?" asks Dr. Rosas.

"The air," his wife replies. "Isn't it too cold?"

Vincentino Rosas gets up and turns off the air conditioner. When he returns to the table, he confesses that his pants have split a seam, and he chuckles. Dona Celeste's face remains passive, while Joana seizes the occasion to propose a toast to the "newlyweds." The maid, an old woman from Trás-os-Montes with eyes like a witch, serves the crème brulée. The state of the nation is discussed: economics, unemployment, politics. At a certain point cousin Arthur, who has yet to say a word, declares that it's all very complicated, "Everything is much too complicated and complex," and this produces a general silence. Everyone stops to look at the hostess. Dona Celeste smiles, and the smile instantly self-destructs.

The talk turns to food, restaurants, bio-products, supermarkets, superstores, shopping malls, central heating, the flu. From there it shifts to Public Figures in Public Places. Vicentino Rosas says he once saw a soccer star in London Plaza. "He had on huge sunglasses and a cowboy hat and seemed much shorter, but I'm sure it was him." No one reacts, and the host insists, "I mean, he was perfectly unrecognizable, but I'll be damned if I didn't recognize him right on the spot!" Everyone laughs uproariously at his cleverness, and Professor Mendes Fernandes says that he once saw Catherine Deneuve in the Thieve's Market. "She seemed interested in the old postcard stand. Could it be the girl understands Portuguese?" Upon hearing "girl," his wife peeks over his shoulder, "Oh Rolando ...." There is a fresh silence, slightly longer than the previous one, and the guests turn their attention to their dessert plates and glasses of wine. The sound of cutlery, dishes, crystal, chewing, sipping, swallowing, after which the woman named Marilia or Marianita says that she once saw the Prime Minister of Portugal running down the street in shorts and sneakers. It was near Restelo, on a Saturday. "He was exercising. I don't mean 'running' in the sense of running away from something, but in the sense of jogging." When she says "jogging," Joana looks over at Americo.

It's a surreptitious glance in the direction of her parents, a sidewise smile that naughty children exchange at the adults' table. A suggestion of mischief that he hasn't seen from her in weeks, in centuries. A slight provocation that might change everything between them—who knows?—maybe back to the way it was in the old days. And how does he react?

Americo concentrates on his reply with intense focus. He forces his upper and lower lips and all the muscles inside his cheeks to form a kind of parentheses, an attempt to create the exact, proper smile to reciprocate Joana's; Joana, the love of his life. But, goddammit, he doesn't possess his mother-in-law's gift for smiling: it makes his eyes hurt; they are much too dry, tearless, the pain builds, as if somewhere inside his head his eyeballs were being stretched from behind by invisible strings—and there inside that head nothing, not one word, not one chance for redemption, reciprocation, only that image—so banal, so forsaken, so naked—of the face of Carla Bruna on the front page of that miserable rag of a newspaper.

A little while later, in the living room, he drinks from a glass of port that Vicentino Rosas has served to his guests and thinks of her. He tries to recall her as a living being, that's how he wants to remember her, as a woman, not a corpse. Some of the guests are seated, others standing; clouds of conversation drift through the room. Next to Americo, Professor Mendes Fernandes elaborates on the new "end of days," a world at once much smaller and much more remote, the perils of capitalism, no longer matters of ideology but matters of metaphysical reality, propped up by a cult of consumerism that is passive to the marrow, the melodrama of a United Nations trapped in the snare of realpolitik and the question of an ever-more-elusive connection between thought and power, philosophy and politics, word and idea, notion and counter-notion, idea and action, the culmination of what he calls "configured man." He goes on dropping names and Americo goes on nodding. In a corner of the room Joana applauds a little flourish that cousin Arthur performs with his fingers. A magic trick of some sort? Americo takes another sip of port. The professor, meanwhile, doesn't stop talking. Ecology, technology, democracy. He looks down at the carpet as if the words had stitched themselves onto its surface: *education, hope, change, mentalities, fundamental, essential.* Countless quotes, a thousand allusions. He says "Arendt" and Americo pictures the cheap room in the pension in Pleasure Plaza, a shabby but ample room, bathed in a diffuse and piquant orange light; he says "Fukuyama" and Americo thinks of Carla Bruna entering the room and looking at him fearlessly as she positions herself on all fours on top of the thick wooden bed, her brown mulatto body looking darker and darker the more he stares at it; he says "Mangabeira Unger" and Americo can smell—is it possible?—her aroma, her singular scent of sun and sex, street and sweat, blood and trees; and when the professor is about to conclude his discourse on old versus new paradigms and, with a stream of quotations that are either too confusing or too erudite for our actor, invokes the names Hayek, Zizek, Keynes, Badiou, Plato, Karl Marx, Americo sees her. It's incredible, but yes, he can actually *see* her. Carla Bruna is alive.

He sees her from behind, crossing from the wall in the living room of his in-laws to God-knows-where, somewhere outside, toward Roma Boulevard, walking on air as if it were nothing, atop the inverted L's of the traffic lights, over the lights of the physical world, swinging her hips with musical authority. As she moves away, she turns back, and, looking at him with an ambiguous smile, entreats him to join her. And he, who suffers from the worst kind of vertigo and has never in his life crossed through a wall of any kind, accepts. Professor Mendes Fernandes asks him, "Do you get what I'm saying?" And he says yes. And, as he raises the glass to his lips, he gets it, yes, he understands.

But there is no wine left in the glass; it is empty.

He aborts the gesture, disguises it as something else. The glass is completely empty and no, there is nothing that can save him: no miracle, no idea, nothing. Carla Bruna is dead.

In the car, on the way home (Joana is driving and Joachim is in the back, asleep in his child seat), he looks at the city through the windshield (walls with windows, walls with holes, joyful, drunk people on the sidewalks, abandoned gardens, the blurred belvedere, red lights, pulsating forms) and realizes that the one appropriate response to all this would be to decisively open the door and, without saying a word, toss himself onto the moving pavement, freeing himself forever from all the imaginings of his wordless body, this mere body known as Americo Abril. But will he do it, or something equally reckless, equally liberating? Or something minimally, vaguely like it?

7. Pleasure Plaza

In the morning, after Joana has left for the Department of Olive Oils, Americo takes Joachim out in his stroller. He stops at the newsstand to read the front pages. There doesn't seem to be anything noteworthy going on in the world, no terrorist attacks or player signings, but Americo takes his time perusing the headlines. He pulls out a banknote and buys five newspapers, from the most prestigious to the most sensational.

He sits in the park and pores over everything: the floods in Asia, the elections in Belgium, the schools in Angola, the UFOs in Entroncamento. Joachim is wide awake in his stroller. He looks upward, with intense concentration, as though the branches framed against the morning sky were a philosophical riddle.

But there is nothing in the newspapers about Carla Bruna. Not a single development concerning what *The Scandal*, in yesterday's edition, referring to the ill-fated "escort," called *Death of The Bod*.

"Let's go then, kid?" says Americo, pushing away his son's stroller. He descends down to Pleasure Plaza, hoping to find something, anything, that will help him make sense of all this. "'Pleasure Plaza.' Such an unfortunate name, don't you think?"

But, amidst the Technicolor breeze that swirls down the street, Joachim only smiles.

The doorman at Club Erox is a gargantuan specimen with no trace of beard or sideburns and with hair so short it looks like it's been sketched on. Americo pushes the stroller towards him, eyes lowered, feigning absentmindedness. "Excuse me ... do you have the time?"

The doorman looks at him, amused. "It's noon, straight up, give or take a few."

Americo smiles along. It's a poker face of a smile, masking a weak hand.

"Do I know you from somewhere? You're not Varela's cousin, by any chance?"

"No."

"Funny, you look a lot alike, helluva lot. And he's got a kid, just like this little one here," the man says, regarding Joachim in the stroller. "Coo-coo! Coo-coo!" he blurts out, suddenly, waving his stubby hands along the side of his face.

But the kid doesn't even blink. What a cool customer. The doorman reels off an entire repertoire of buffoonery—wagging his ears, lurching his eyebrows, hurling out the most idiotic monosyllables—trying to extract a laugh, a sound, the slightest smile—but the kid doesn't move a muscle. He remains as inscrutable and serene as the wisest Buddha.

"You're not amused, are you?" asks the doorman, sweating. The question is rhetorical, the sweat literal.

Americo apologizes, says that as a rule his son is quite good-natured, he's just a little sleepy today, he didn't sleep very well last night, he's been stuffed up, it's almost time for his nap. After he says this he glances at the door behind the man and adds, as though it meant nothing, "Pretty crazy what happened the other day ..."

But the doorman is intrigued by the boy who won't laugh. "How old is he?"

"Him? He's a year."

"That's all?"

"Just over a year-and-a-half, actually."

Joachim looks up at the two adults. One he recognizes as his father, the other … no clue. He doesn't like the way they just stand there looking at him.

"Now I remember," says Americo. "Isn't this the place where that thing with the call girl happened?"

"You're quite the little man, aren't you?" The doorman ignores the question. He squats beside the stroller and tries to catch Joachim's attention.

Joachim takes a deep, dramatic breath. He lifts his eyebrows, lowers his lips, then opens his mouth wide—so wide it looks like a Greek mask—and lets loose a terrible shriek.

Americo rocks the stroller. "Shh, it's okay, it's okay …."

But Joachim squeals mercilessly.

"Come on," says Americo, feeling the blood rush to his face. "Be quiet now." He can sense the silent judgment of the crass doorman. It was here, by this very door, on a stormy night a little more than two years ago, that he first met Carla Bruna. "Can you pay me in vodka?" she said. He burns with shame. The doorman stares at him; he is thinking, for sure, that he is an imbecile, a weakling, a lousy father, the dolt of all dolts.

"Come on, Joachim, don't do this," he repeats, rocking the stroller harder now, his despair more pronounced, while keeping one eye fixed on the doorman, who appears to be shaking his head and saying, "Tsk tsk." Tsk Tsk? What a cretin. What right does he have to feel superior, to reproach and diminish him? Goddamit, this is too much. Americo stops rocking the stroller. How much does a guy have to take, after all? Determined to teach the sideburn-less lunatic a lesson, he lifts his head, looks him right in the eyes. He'll sketch with his fists what's missing on that face.

"Doesn't he have a pacifier?" asks the doorman.

"What?" Americo says. "Oh … yeah, sure." He pulls the pacifier out of his pocket and sticks it in his son's mouth.

And, *voila*, he shuts up.

How shameful, the kid shuts up ... immediately. "Well, uh, thank you very much," his father, pathetic clown, says, and pushes the stroller away.

He can hear, still, the doorman in the distance. "See ya next time! And *ciao* to you, little Joey Keester!"

Making fun of a little kid. His defenseless little child who isn't responsible for his name—the name that he and Joana, together, gave him. A name, incidentally, that's not all that uncommon, such as it is. A quite traditional Portuguese name, a serious and dignified and beautiful name. What an ignoramus, this second-rate doorman, who is he to judge him? He's got elbows growing out of his head, the fuck. Muscles up to his gums, a total pissing knuckle-dragger. His words echo in Americo's brain: "And *ciao* to you, little Joey Keester! Aren't you Varela's cousin? Such a little man. Doesn't he have a pacifier?" He could strangle him with his own hands.

Pushing the stroller up the boulevard, he feels a tightness in his chest. A pain he doesn't recognize, as if someone were pushing a cabinet full of shoes up against his heart. Could he be having a heart attack? He stops in the street, sits down by a fire hydrant and cries like a baby.

Passersby stare at him. What a pathetic tableau: the silent son and the sobbing father. When he calms down, Americo pulls out his cell phone and makes a decision. He deletes all of Carla Bruna's texts. And the only one that he sent her, my God, the day before she—just one day before she—before *that. XXX?* Is that all there is? We live and we live and then one day we die?

Joachim looks at him from the stroller, utterly beaming. How funny, the little drops of water, spiraling down his father's face.

In his dream Americo is on the street, facing a wall, reading the newspaper. The wall, or partition, has the odor of fresh paint. It's an aroma that transports him back to childhood. He reads on the inside pages the news about the murder of Carla Bruna. A high-resolution photograph (a true "work of art," he thinks in the dream) shows her crumpled, twisted body, half on the bed and half off it. Her head hangs down, almost touching the floor, her legs are pressed against the wall. Her naked breast, at once lighter and darker than the rest of her body (how odd), is visible, but fortunately she's wearing panties. Americo reads the news as if he already knows it all, as if it doesn't really affect him. Passing strangers peer over his shoulder trying to see what he is reading, and Americo hides it from view. He bought the newspaper; it's for him to read. The pages are of a vague pink color with austere graphics and museum-worthy photography like those of the *Financial Times*. There is no sign of a wound on Carla Bruna's body, but her face is sliced up, gashed, rutted beyond recognition. "Carla Bruna." So that was indeed her real name. Americo is looking at the overturned lamp in the photo when he senses a presence lurking behind him. He turns; it's the Doorman. The man doesn't speak, he simply stares at him blankly: the look of an absolute moron. It's enough for Americo to know everything: he's the culprit. It was he who killed my Bruna, my love; he who did the evil deed; he who obliterated her forever. "Son of a motherfucking bitch," he says, before grabbing him by the neck and throwing him to the floor with untold force. His big square head cracks against the cobblestones, pow, bam. Blood gushes from his nostrils and ears like in a low-budget horror flick, his eyes go even more vacant than usual. Americo hovers over him like a Justice League superhero. "I didn't mean to offend you," murmurs the Doorman, "There must be some misunderstanding. I didn't wish to offend …." But Americo has already drawn the Swiss Army knife from his pocket, unloosed the blade, and begun slicing up his face. Wielding it like a sculptor, he attempts to replicate, from memory, the exact gashes he saw in the photo of Carla Bruna. The Doorman squeals like a pig but he couldn't care less. He performs his task with the serenity of a surgeon.

He has shut out everything else, there is only this, this face and this blade, slicing as it goes, slicing what he remembers. Start at the left eyebrow and descend diagonally, severing the mouth in two. A nice hole ... in the cheek. Cut the nose ... here ...

Now the blood begins to spurt, overflowing from the man's face like dirty water in a rumpus room on the day of a national flood, and Americo perceives the time has come to stop. There are no features left to see, no details left to ascertain. A great noise arises—a chorus of voices, shoes, scraps of words. There is a mob approaching—a throng, a city—to apprehend him, to take him away. My God. Americo drops the blade and rises to his feet. His hands are covered with blood. In a final moment of freedom, he sees the open newspaper hovering over the pavement. Yes, hovering, just like in one of those lovely photographs from a war scene, a catastrophe, of a child playing amongst the rubble of a devastated school; or a random dove, staggering atop a pile of charred corpses; or a light, for instance, a miraculous light, piercing the evil clouds of an explosion. And, at this moment, he awakens.

It's just a dream. He has tortured and killed the culprit in a dream, just a dream. But he feels so much stronger now.

In the morning, he opens the window that looks to the sky out back and prepares a proper breakfast. An old-fashioned meal: toast with butter and jam, scrambled eggs with salt and pepper, orange juice, and a good cup of coffee with milk. He sits at the table to indulge in the precious peace and quiet but is interrupted by his wife. "Oh, so here you are."

"Leaving already?" he says.

"I'm late," she says, and takes some fat-free Greek liquid yogurt from the fridge.

So composed, so impeccably dressed, so get-up-and-go. Americo looks at her and feels like he's inside some kind of lousy TV commercial. A slow-motion shot of his modern wife taking the product, opening it, then bringing it to her mouth with the utmost elegance— the fine blond silhouette of his very own Joaninha Maria de Miranda Rosas, meticulously framed by the light of the fridge, drinking that one-of-a-kind yogurt that not only provides a day's worth of energy but also slims and protects the body from any number of theoretical maladies—all overlaid with music, which Americo recognizes from somewhere, a dream, perhaps, growing closer, more forceful, less musical, devolving into one shrill, piercing note, a noise, until Joana turns toward him and, abandoning the character of the Yogurt Lady, says: "Can't you hear Joachim?"

It's not a question; it's an order. Americo plays dumb for one, two, three seconds, then gets up.

"Bye my dears!" shouts Joana, full of good cheer, as she heads off to work. She slams the door—*bam!*—while he goes to change his son's diaper.

Reclining on the sofa, observing a philosophical discussion between Joachim and a stuffed giraffe, Americo looks at the cell phone vibrating in his hand. He doesn't recognize the number.

"Hello? Who is it?"

"Americo Abril?"

"Yes?"

"My name is Susana Monterrança, I'm a journalist with *Oh! Daily*, and I would like to ask you some questions about the so-called 'Death of The Bod' case. The case of that chorus girl at Club Erox who showed up dead last Thursday. Do you know of what I speak?"

He can't believe it.

"Hello? Can you hear me? Americo Abril, are you hearing me OK?"

" ... Uh ... what?"

"I was asking you if you've heard about the 'Death of The Bod' case."

"I'm ... not ... hearing ... you very well ... you sound ... far off .... I'm just going into a tunnel, I think I'm losing the signal. ... Hello, can you hear me?" shouts the actor, pulling away from the cell phone. "Hello? He-llo? Can you hea—." He hangs up.

On the floor, amidst the chaos of red, yellow and blue toys, Joachim regards him with an open mouth. Man as an interrogative beast.

"It's all right," Americo tells him. "Don't be afraid, everything's all right."

He vomits up his magnificent breakfast in the bathroom. All of it a chewed-up, squashed, swallowed, spat-up jumble—eggjam, orange-milk—a horrid, unrecognizable confection, this can't be, this just cannot be, dearjesusgod. No, a telephone call from a journalist is not good. Why on Earth did that woman call here to ask that question? Americo leans against the wall, tries to calm himself. He hears his son crying far off in the other room. He's starving, he has to fix him something to eat. He has to clean up this frightful mess that his digestive system wrought on the floor and on the edges of the toilet and act like a grown man, get up and run to the kitchen and fix his son something to eat. Get up and ... "I'm coming, Joachim! Don't cry, I'm coming!" Oh no, here comes another puke. "Daddy's coming, dear!"

8. To Sleep

At the end of the day, Joana arrives home bursting with energy, seized by her usual frenetic fatigue, entangled in a dream that doesn't quite know where it ends or begins, her arms flailing, jabbering endlessly, talking in that astounding and somewhat frightful manner that manages to render anything—an out-of-place paper, a stain on the wall, a child's belch—a topic of discourse, proceeding to remake the world, at least, that is, the tiny world of her private domain. Transfiguring it ever so slightly, reordering everything, all this tiny tactile reality into a great fictive mass of babble and thin air; anyway, that's the effect it has on Americo, this voracious vertiginous verbosity (VVV) with which Joana treats everyday life, suffusing everything with such hot air that Americo wonders that the house itself doesn't float away like a helium balloon.

But today he's going to tell her. He's going to tell her everything, he will not let the day pass without telling her. His carnal affair with Carla Bruna, the news of Carla Bruna's homicide, the phone call from the journalist about Carla Bruna. He can no longer cope with this burden, this lie, this unceasing recoiling remorse. It will all explode, one way or another; it's better he tell her now. Show sincere remorse, get choked up, tell her to take it easy, that he still loves her, that they must think of Joachim. All of which, in its way, is the truth.

"Today, you can't imagine …," she says.

He can imagine all right; as always she's about to tell one of her olive oil stories. He can't let her go on. The moment has come. He has to tell her everything, before she reels off the thousand and twenty-nine bureaucratic issues raised today at the National Department of Quality Control of Olive Oils. Here he goes. But what, what to say, and how? Where to begin? And with which words?

"What?" he asks, just to gain a few precious seconds.

"You can't imagine," says Joana. "You can't even imagine. We were all at our desks, doing our work, minding our own business, quietly looking at our computer screens, the oldest in all of Europe, those ugly green screens that have got to be just awful for the eyes, who knows, those machines must run on coal, you press a key and you hear a noise from the things, this forced mechanical groan, *vroom, vroom,* and after you have to wait an eternity for the page to change, you just can't imagine, but, so anyway, there we are, yes, doing our work, God only knows what a colossal, tedious pain in the ass it all is, and suddenly, guess who appears at the door, the Deputy Director, but not my boss, the Amilcar I'm always talking about, no, not him, he's the Regional Deputy Director, this is the Deputy Director of *everyone,* the National Deputy Director, a tall bald guy with tufts of hair on the sides of his head, combed outward, or, rather, *uncombed* in God-knows- what direction, as if he had just gone through a hurricane on the main elevator, whatever, anyway so this guy just appears out of nowhere, in a tie and a suit so big you could take a swim inside it, with one of those really thin wrinkly old goosenecks with all that loose skin hanging down, but, anyway, the guy shows up, makes some gesture for everyone to stay seated, and in an old, shaky voice, he declares that 'As of today, anyone who breaches, delays, or boycotts an order from above ceases to have rights in this organization. As should be evident, none of you heard this, so it's not necessary to go blabbing about that which I didn't say to anyone outside of these four walls. Thank you very much, work well, stay well ....' Anyway, something like that, give or take a comma or two. He drops this incredible bomb, then turns around and splits. Vanishes just like that. Do you see, do you see what all this has come to, what an unbelievable, absolutely unbelievable point all this crap has come to?"

"Yeah," says Americo, deciding not to tell her anything just now. "Unbelievable …."

Together they bathe Joachim, dry Joachim, rub lotion on Joachim, feed Joachim, change Joachim's diaper, put Joachim to bed, and then, exhausted, collapse on the sofa in front of the television.

There's a medical drama on the tube. A hospital somewhere in America where life-and-death cases raise ethical, political, and emotional questions. In one scene a clown hired to cheer up a patient slips on the staircase and bleeds from his buttock. In another scene a very pretty girl of sixteen or seventeen lies in bed in a private room, reading a book and smiling. A doctor, holding her test results in his hand, stops to look at her through the window glass. He carries a burden: enter the room, interrupt her reading, and tell her she's going to die in a few weeks. Close-up of the doctor biting his lip. Cut to a tighter close-up of the doctor's eyes—black, nearly black, intensely focused: the sadness, the fear, the doubt. "Fuck," he says. As misfortune would have it, the chief physician appears at that very moment. "What did you say?" he asks, as if he hadn't heard it. "Fuck!" repeats the young doctor, turning halfway around. In the room the doomed girl lifts her eyes from the book to see what is going on outside the window. The chief physician meets her eyes and returns a restrained, professional smile. Of course the viewer knows it's a sad smile. The young girl resumes her reading, serene, almost happy. "Hey, where are you going?" the chief shouts to the doctor, distancing himself, drifting down the corridor. "I will not tolerate this kind of language in my hospital!" But the young doctor ignores him and continues walking until he vanishes. Other doctors, interns, and nurses stop in their tracks, awaiting the chief's reaction. But he just stands there, frozen in place, breathing. Suddenly he's a graceless and very old man. A little man in a large building. "Don't they understand?" he says.

Later, in bed, Americo thinks that perhaps the young doctor was right not to speak. Perhaps it's best not to reveal everything, not to tell the truth if the truth isn't so great. The great lesson of adulthood, learning when to say nothing.

Alongside him, propped against a pillow, Joana reads *The Temptation of the Golden Talents*, a crime novel set in 33 A.D. If he told her about his infidelities with Carla Bruna, would she suffer? She'd suffer some, for sure, but how much, exactly? How much, more or less, on a scale of one to ten? An eight? A six? A four? A five? On the other hand, isn't it always better to tell the truth? After the initial shock passed, wouldn't everything between them become that much easier? The truth. To tell the whole truth, cautiously, but without distorting or omitting anything, wouldn't that, in the end, be the most benign solution, the least bloody for everyone?

Americo sits up in bed. He does not want to be lying down on the marital bed at the very moment he confesses to his wife that he's been secretly screwing The Bod. "Is everything okay with you?" he asks.

"Everything, sure. And with you?"

He doesn't respond. He combs back his hair, he doesn't know why, and straightens the pillow behind his back. It's important, in big moments like this, to maintain the proper posture, a posture that conveys security, certainty, composure, one that doesn't suggest ulterior motives or any sort of duplicity. He looks at his wife, engrossed in the Biblical thriller, and thinks of what words to use. "Put down the book, please, Joana. There is something I have to tell you." Or: " ... a *serious* thing to tell you"? "An *important* thing"? "An *awful* thing"? No, just "something." "There is something I have to tell you," and then say it. The truth. Simple as that. He looks at her. Here goes: "Joana?"

She throws herself at him, clamps his mouth between her cold lips, a parched pair of lips that make him long for the fiery lips of dead Carla, then sits on him and snatches off her nightshirt, revealing her skinny white body, perhaps a little too skinny, a quality that America, oddly enough, has no memory of whatsoever, good or bad, and glimpses, out of the corner of his eye, the bestseller left open on the bed sheet, a purple tome with shiny gold coins on the cover. *The Temptation of the Golden Talents*, that thing, that object just lying there, at that moment seeming suddenly sinister and dirty, a piece of filth atop the white sheets on which they sleep and dream their intimate dreams, while Joana, eyes closed, rocks back and forth, back and forth, thrusting backward and forward between their past of languid weekends walking hand-in-hand on the beach and her radiant future as Regional Deputy Director of Olive Oils or maybe even Adjunct to the National Deputy Director or perhaps, who knows, Managing National Deputy Director With Special Powers Of Direct Delegatory Negotiations For All Matters Relative To Olive Oils And Its Derivatives, Etc., and as she rocks back and forth, so lovingly, so purposefully above him, he lies beneath her, pressed into his guilt, admiring her pointy breasts.

On Tuesday, an e-mail arrives with the revised screenplay of *Being Paul Giamatti*. Americo is unnerved after reading the ninety-nine new pages. It's still the story of an actor named Giamatti who, due to a glitch, a misunderstanding at a computer store, ends up trapped inside a video game called *Being Alive* that is exactly the same as his real life. The same, but with one tiny difference: the game does not end with his death. The game ends when he actually *becomes* Paul Giamatti. That is, when he becomes "himself." Presented like this it sounds almost philosophical, but it's all much simpler in the script. Way too simple; moronic, in fact. In order to become more "himself" (and, presumably, in order to exit the game and return to the outside world), our protagonist Giamatti must solve the problems that surround him, thereby gaining awareness of his own capabilities and limitations. In Level One, he finds himself trapped in the body of a squat, bald Columbian (but with little resemblance to the actual Paul Giamatti), living illegally in the United States of America. In Level Two he is himself, Americo. And this is where, in the new version rewritten for the European shoots, the story has been altered. Now the story of Americo's Giamatti begins at an airport. He's killing time between flights, after having arrived from Bogota following an unlikely series of events (he was bitten by a Filipino flight attendant and dragged into the smoked-glass booth of the Office of Foreign Citizens and Border Security for a "naked interrogation" conducted by two agents "stinking of cynicism and stupor"), and, having had an epiphany on a toilet in an airport restroom while reciting obscure classical verses in Spanish and chanting dubious laments ending in "oh" or in "ayy," he decided that, yes, he needed to change his life and, yes, he would drop in the water—*ploosh!*—the bags of cocaine he had smuggled all these thousands of kilometers from Bogota "stuffed up his ass," forbidden bags worth a fortune in this country—pristinely white, intensely white bags—shimmering as if lit from within, bags shaped like sausages undetectable by X-ray scanners, door frame alarms, zealous customs agents, suspicious detectives and even two sleepy German shepherds. By tossing these bags in the—*ploosh!*—toilet, flushing them—*fpshhhhh!*—down, our hero reveals himself finally disposed to accept the miracle of his *being*, the "redemption that each of us carries in his heart like an internal recovery disk," whereupon a solemn, pervasive soundtrack kicks in (Mozart? Pink Floyd?) and he transforms into Americo, a tiny Second-Level Giamatti. Fantastic. Now the other is already himself and he is seated next to Door D46 with an antique suitcase at his feet, waiting to board the flight to Portugal, when an extremely pale and extremely blond woman dressed in a black skirt and black boots and black leather sits in a chair directly in front of him. Giamatti pretends to try to remove the remainder of a sticker on his suitcase but can't manage to look away from her. The woman, who could very well be the personification of Death or of Evil right out of a contemporary theater production, leafs through a magazine with photographs of out-of-focus kings and topless queens. Every now and then, like someone absentmindedly tossing a bomb, she lifts her right eyebrow and crosses and uncrosses her legs, causing her skirt to rise up higher. Or she smiles in a way that Giamatti finds much too sophisticated as to have been inspired by anything in the frivolous rag she's reading. Or she grazes, with two fingers, ever so lightly, a certain key spot in the triangle of her neckline, a surgically precise gesture that at once intensifies the geometry of the triangle, educes the aroma off her body, and enhances the menace of the cleavage. She's a *femme fatale*, this is nothing to her; she does it all the time. Giamatti looks around, in search of other foci, any potential distraction, but his eyes keep pulling him in the same direction. He scratches himself, combs whatever hair remains on the sides of his head, fidgets in his chair, coughs.

The woman doesn't even look up.

His interest eventually wanes and he falls asleep. (Close-up of the snoring bald man.)

"Paul Giamatti?"

He opens his eyes. Startled from sleep, he trembles, eyes bulging. Standing right in front of him, the woman in black. "Wha—?"

She says, "I have a little secret for you," grabs him by the hand, leads him into the ladies' room. They lock themselves inside a stall, climb atop a toilet, so no one can see their feet beneath the door, and undress. What happens between the two of them stays between the two of them, as it should. Meanwhile the deafening racket of jet engines is heard and the camera becomes independent of the characters, fixing on the long rectangular mirror over the washbasins and, in an elaborate trick of cinematic chicanery, zooms in on the reflective surface without us seeing any part of the camera or the cameraman. Zooming in gradually, it is the perspective of an invisible man fearfully approaching the blankness of his own image. And, when we return to our little stall of *amour*, what we encounter is: death!

The blond woman in black is dead. There is no sign of a wound, no blood; it's a matter of internal bleeding. Giamatti looks at her, stricken dumb with disillusion, sorrow, fear, paranoia, and heartache (in that order). He leaves her sitting on the commode, tries to balance her head against the flush handle. After several attempts he finally succeeds. When he looks at her for the last time she seems much paler. Blanched skin, black clothing: a dead woman in mourning.

"Pardon me," he says to the corpse. "I don't know what went wrong here but ... I'm really quite sorry."

He leaves scratching his head, like a student leaving an exam with minimal expectations. When he reaches the bathroom exit, he stops, turns, goes back. He peeks into the stall.

"I very much enjoyed ... learning ... your ... secret," he says, before running away.

And, as if in response (a response that he misses but that we, the audience, see), the head of the dead woman falls to one side.

Leaning against Door D46, Giamatti looks around, sits back in his chair. He sighs. He now has an objective. "I have an objective," he mutters softly, as if he were praying. "I have a purpose, to become myself entirely." But how, dear God, to achieve it? The suitcase is still where he left it. No one has touched it; no international thief, none of those security guys that blow up neglected packages. That bloody old suitcase; it's really quite hideous.

Trying to calm down, or pretending to, anyway, Giamatti leans backward on the chair and crosses his arms. For no reason at all, as a guise, perhaps, as a diversion, he watches the people passing through the corridor of the boarding area. He follows them with his eyes, searching for—what?—something different, something meaningful, some kind of *clue*. Yes, this is good. He feels like he's inside a tale of high espionage, seeking an assassin, someone dangerous, someone all too quiet, some malevolent sign.

But he all sees are normal folks pushing carts filled with luggage, shopping bags, surfboards, chocolates. Giamatti gives up the game.

He shifts his gaze downward, toward the floor, to his feet, to the inside of his head. It seems the sequence of his consternation was incomplete. It should have been: disillusion, sorrow, fear, paranoia, heartache, and guilt.

In the immense airport he digs his poorly trimmed nails into his face, tearing the skin; pulls at his cheeks with great, terrible force, with all the force he can muster, until the pain becomes intolerable and tears, monstrously fat tears, fall—*plop!*—onto his yellow sneakers.

In the afternoon Americo drops Joachim off at Mother's house. His mother tries to tell him about her recent antique shop adventure, a hilarious misunderstanding involving a Greek gemstone that she wanted, yet didn't really want, but Americo tells her he's late for a meeting, a vitally important engagement. His mother perceives, of course, that something isn't quite right, that there is something false beneath the smiling evasions of her son's demeanor. She understands it quite well but doesn't bother to protest. She doesn't even ask when he's coming back to pick up his child, doesn't ask about "Little Joanie," doesn't comment on the haggard state of his appearance. How does he expect to ever be offered a spot on another *telenovela* with those deep, dark circles under his eyes and the slaughtered-lamb look on his face? The only question she doesn't neglect to ask is whether he's visited his father this month.

"I'll go tomorrow," Americo says. "Tomorrow or the day after, at the latest."

"Don't you forget."

"Of course not, Mother. I never forget."

She looks at him in silence, a silence he reciprocates, for as long as he can stand it. Then he lowers his head and smiles. It's a lie, of course.

Half an hour later, Americo is downing beers and eating salted peanuts in Murilo's living room. They talk about soccer, interest rates, restaurants, and, after a while, on the second round of beers, he begins telling his friend the story of Carla Bruna. He tells it as if it were just another story of the night, no different than those Murilo tells every week, interspersing the narrative with macho jokes and redeeming it with coarse language, and, in the most difficult parts, attempting to find some measure of commonality in the tragedy. He says "a girl from Club Erox"; he says "with all the goods"; he says, "It's unimaginable; they murdered her." He doesn't say "Carla Bruna"; he doesn't say "my love"; he doesn't say "the pain, the guilt, the burning fires of hell." He notes, in passing, that there was even a mention of it in the papers, but doesn't elaborate further. He is unsure whether to reveal the telephone call from the journalist. "You know, the problem is …"

But at that exact moment the bastard gets up. "Another cold one?"

"Yeah … good idea," Americo replies. And he stands there, alone, trying to pick tiny pieces of peanut from his teeth.

When Murilo returns with the beers, he flies in all charged up and talking in rounded tones about Marietta, some knockout that, ahh, you can only imagine, "one of those girls that, you know, dude, must have only existed in Nabokov's day, know what I mean?" Americo nods, yeah he can just imagine, and smiles—tentatively, generously, irreproachably—like a true friend. And says nothing more.

The good part is, when he falls asleep, his dreams have nothing do to with any of this.

In a foreign city a flock of chickens resolve to throw themselves off the roof of a skyscraper. They are ten, fifteen, twenty well-cared-for creatures, very fat and very white, left there by someone with a cruel streak. A comic little bunch, but this is not a moment for levity. One of the chickens stretches her neck upward, the others turn towards her, pick up the signal, divine its meaning. And off they go, waddling on their comedic feet like Chaplin towards the edge of the building and a certain death. Americo feels a kind of inchoate anguish over the fate of the doomed fowl; his afflicted heart strains. He has this thought within the dream: *I don't want to look, no, I can't look*. But he has no choice; he is stuck inside his own head. And what he sees is a miracle: the chicken flies, the goddamned chicken flies! First, the leader with the stretched neck, then the others. Against the blue sky of winter, they fly with unexpected grace, the whole flock of them. Irredeemably white, they seem like swans or flying rays. Impossible notions, gentle sensations, bliss. How good it is to sleep.

For an entire week, Americo sticks to this plan: Whenever any disquiet or sense of guilt threatens to take hold, whenever any sort of shadow appears on the horizon, hovers over his head, he drinks two glasses of wine and, *voilà*, problem solved. He lies down to sleep and everything vanishes. The glorious "restorative sleep" of the ancients.

He dreams often of white creatures. Lambs, rabbits, gulls, zebras without stripes. The dreams don't always end as well as the skyscraper-chickens one. With the lambs there is always blood, of course, which detracts somewhat from the restorative nature of the siesta.

One day Americo awakens quite troubled, confusing the half-light of his room with the empty pallor of death, the decapitated lamb in his dream with his real and innocent son—and runs to Joachim's room to feel his pulse, to listen to his breathing, to watch over him for a few minutes just to make certain that, yes, he is only sleeping and everything is just fine; Joachim has suffered nothing horrible on account of his father's guilt, on account of his father's anguish, on account of the bloody lambs that scamper through his father's dreams.

On other occasions, he remembers nothing upon waking. The dreams are much too dark.

But today is different. Today Americo resists the temptations of both wine and sleep. He can't go on like this; he has to move forward, involve himself in some activity, do something. He sits in his room and thinks. In front of him, the purple painting that Joana bought from an artist friend for a truckload of cash. A splatter of purple.

Americo never quite got it. A lousy smear of purple? Since nothing is coming to him, he turns on the television.

Clutching the wing of a military jet in midflight, the heartthrob hero pulls out his cell phone, calls a scientist, and asks for advice. The frenzied sky dishevels his hair in the most flattering way, but our heartthrob hero doesn't even blink. He wields the cell phone like a modern-day machete. Suddenly, the sound of keys, a door opening—instinctively Americo snatches the remote and turns off the TV—and in walks Joana with her voracious vertiginous verbosity (VVV).

She says that she never buys a newspaper, she doesn't like reading newspapers, that newspapers are finished and that's fine by her, they are objects from another time, almost always poorly designed, poorly arranged, and dirty, she says that she never reads newspapers because, deep inside, she's a little superstitious—"Aren't we all?"—and thinks, or suspects, or fears that to know about the world is to invite disaster, that to know about things is to know about bad things, and for this reason, when she can't avoid picking up a newspaper, and she opens it, reads the headlines, the briefs, the classifieds, looks at the photographs, she always feels a strange, malevolent shiver, as if she were guilty of some secret, of some gruesome thing, and reading the news was a way of exposing herself to the revelation of that original sin. Americo looks at her, awestruck. This is his wife to a tee: a soliloquy without a breath, without a resolution, full of rhetorical questions and useless repetitions. But the content isn't usually so heavy. He stands up and, with the dispassionate cool of a pickpocket in a police station, lays the remote on the sofa. So that his wife doesn't notice that he's been watching TV in the middle of the afternoon. As a matter of fact, it is a bit odd for her to be home at this hour. It's not customary for his bureaucrat-wife to leave work so early. But, just when he's about to ask her about this, Joana flattens him again with her notorious VVV.

She tells him it's cold, that it's cold but there's a sun, that she so loves the autumn sun, that, well, it's not quite autumn but still she can sense its presence, that over the last hour, during these last few minutes when she was driving home, she felt more than she has felt in ages, more emotions, more certitude mixed with doubt—"Could this be an actual emotion?"—and, upon saying this, she redirects her gaze toward the painting on the wall where there is nothing but purple, a weird amalgam of purple and pink and, turning to face it, says that she's read some books, some classic books in practical psychology and day-to-day spirituality and those that ask the principal questions about happiness in the modern world, but nobody ever told her that life would be like this, that Time is a teacher, that Time is indeed a teacher, that Time will always be a teacher, but, well, it's also a—and a word slips out that sounds like "shit"—but that cannot, of course, be, no it couldn't be "shit," it just couldn't be, the Joana that Americo knows would never say this, maybe "shill" or "spit," or maybe (and this is much more likely) it was an equivocation between the two words that resolved itself in a sound that came out like "shit"—as she says this, or whatever it is she said, she pauses, or suffers some sort of gasp, as if she had stumbled upon something horribly funny about the purple smudge, and all of a sudden—*zap!*—she begins speaking even faster, spewing out words, sentences, paragraphs at an unthinkable velocity, a supersonic, frightening VVV, and, still wearing her jacket and still wielding her purse, shielding herself behind a prodigious smile, says that she just bumped into a childhood friend in Such-and-Such Restaurant, that this lady friend of hers is now bald but unburdened and happy, that they both agreed that it didn't seem like a decade had passed since they last saw each other, that they both ordered the same asparagus salad with the grandiose name, that they both threw ceremony and caution and sense to the wind and ordered one of the most expensive wines on the list, a whole bottle of it, because, after all, it was a special occasion, and, in the middle of the lunch, between the "oil-purged asparagus with a mushroom reduction sprinkled with Azorean pepper" and the "freshwater trout with a dusting of mint crushed by polished antique pebbles," her childhood friend tells her that she doesn't want to worry her and asks her if she's seen the news, and Joana asks why, and her friend says perhaps she shouldn't have mentioned it, perhaps she shouldn't say anything, but now that she has she must, and proceeds to tell her about the news she read on the first page of one of the country's leading tabloids, and Joana turns all pale but plays it cool, says that, yes, of course she knew about it, and that it's all a lie, these rags invent things just to sell more copies, but her friend knows she's lying, and she knows that her friend knows she's lying, and from then on the lunch is a disconsolate affair with no possible salvation, nothing tastes like anything, neither the expensive wine nor the freshwater trout nor the "polar bear osso bucco with southern Lapland huckleberries" that the maître d' has brought over for dessert, and when she gets back to work, Joana sits herself down at the computer and, peering around as if she were about to commit a crime, Googles the tabloid her friend mentioned and reads this: "Actor Maintained Ongoing Affair With Murdered Call Girl," and a chill passes through her like none she's ever known, a gust, a surreal blast of wind that leaves her heart and lungs and all those things we have hanging loose within us, leaves everything suspended and aquiver, "Because, do you know," she says, "do you know, Americo, who the actor was in the newspaper?"

9. Ugly Swear Words

In a scene of rank melodrama, Americo is kicked out of the house, to the screams of his wife, stumbling down the staircase while twisting his neck to look back upwards, afraid that his beloved Joana might hurl his suitcase and his clothes and all his belongings right onto the head of her poor unfaithful husband. And, behind it all, a silent, monochromatic melancholy, completely unrelated to Joana's screams, Joana's hysterics, and the terribly ugly swear words issuing from Joana's delicate lips. No, it's much worse. After all those days and nights feeding him that beige-green slop, changing his smelly diapers, putting up with his pigheadedness, his whims, his tantrums, his unintelligible babbling, Americo hears it quite distinctly: Joachim says his very first word—the virgin word, the seminal word, the historic word, the word that no one will ever forget—and that word is: "Mama?"

How can life be so bloody cruel?

Americo runs fleeing to his mother's house.

He looks downward to avoid catching eyes with anyone and concentrates on his breathing. He's got to make it to her house. Fifteen minutes that seem like fifteen kilometers. As if he were running in place, as if the city were receding away from him. Everything—the facades, the streets—looks so sick. Everything looks so dead.

As he summons the courage to ring the doorbell his mother opens the door, a sermon etched onto her face. Americo asks her if she's heard. "Unfortunately," she says. Americo figures that she must have read the horrible story in the newspaper and tells her he doesn't want to discuss it, that he just needs a place to spend the night. But his mother keeps talking, tells him to calm down, to think about "what you have done, Americo." She takes Joana's side and won't let him explain.

"Mother, in that case I won't even take off my jacket," he says, frowning. It's only a threat, but his mother doesn't shut up and he realizes he has no choice but to leave.

"Maybe you can still work things out!" he hears her yelling from the doorway, loud enough for all of Lisbon to hear. "Think of little Joachim!"

A drunk, leaning against the ATM, sings the national anthem. A convertible packed with laughing girls drives past. A blank, listless, depressing sky hangs over everything.

Americo ends up on Murilo's couch playing the part of the misunderstood schoolboy. He holds his face in his hands, assumes the role of the sufferer—angry with the world, with fate, with everything; detested by everyone. Murilo brings him a glass of wine and tells him that this time he needs to find himself a really good lawyer.

"What about you?"

"I mean a *serious* lawyer," Murilo repeats, watching the line of runway models strutting on the television. Skinny women in complicated hats.

"Thanks, man. You're the only one I can count on."

"Oh, come now, no need to thank me; what's all this? But look, right now, if you could, by chance, I wonder if ... I could ask you to, if you don't mind, go out for a few hours, would you mind? It's just that I'm expecting Juraya ... you know, the one I told you about the other day, the windsurfing chick, the one with the thick cord and great sails? It wouldn't upset you too much, would it?

"Uh, no," Americo says. An intense light emanates from the television set. Long legs and fake smiles. "Of course not, it's fine. I'll just go for a walk, get some air, clear my head …."

Heading down the new streets toward the old quarter, Americo sees himself from above, wandering aimlessly, not knowing where to put his arms. All around him the flimsy lines of the buildings from the sixties and seventies give way to the sturdier ones of the previous two centuries. Just like in one of those old two-reelers where the scenery shifts behind the protagonist, changing as he moves forward; at once a physical and emotional backdrop. As if he were the city itself, and vice versa.

He stops when he gets to Merces. He realizes he's been walking towards his house, carried along on automatic feet. Cars roar past, making a terrible racket, while he stands there, scratching his head on the sidewalk like the poor Giamatti in the movie. He sees himself in the role of the outcast, the penitent, the pitiful schmuck without a shred of dignity. Unshaven, unkempt, malodorous, sleeping in the staircase of his building, in front of door No. 81, waiting for his wife to leave or come back from work just for the privilege of glimpsing her for a few seconds. Praying that, once in a while, she, or some nanny she's hired, will take his child for a walk, so that Americo can see him, so he can make funny faces or wave cheerful good-byes to make him laugh. Hoping his boy still remembers him, hoping he doesn't grow up feeling ashamed and afraid of his own father. But calm down now, there's no need to exaggerate, this is your first day out of the house.

"I love you, girl."

"Happy the idiots and the savage beasts."

"What capital conducts, capitalism fucks."

He gazes at the graffiti on the walls of the Bairro Alto. The murmur of strange voices, trash on the street corners. There is a brutal kind of poetry in walking alone. Whenever he gets close to his house, to door No. 81, 4-D, behind which his dear Joachim must certainly be asleep, behind which his wife, perhaps, is finishing up a report, a recommendation, a reprimand with a distracted smile, seated, perhaps, at her light wooden writing desk from the 1950s, the one with three sizes of drawers—for extra-large, medium, and small-sized secrets, under, perhaps, the molten light of the green banker's lamp, dressed, perhaps, in that thick terry-cloth robe with nothing on underneath—whenever he approaches that cursed door No. 81, Americo knows he shouldn't go there. He repeats it to himself twice, three times. Too many times, in fact, as if to someone who cannot be convinced.

Don't go there. Do not go there.

At Rossio Plaza, he comes across a crowd dressed in white smocks; thousands of people holding lit candles in a sign of protest. A petite woman with Picassoesque eyes gazes at him in silence. She is holding up a placard, "Health Care Workers' Vigil Against Evil." Americo shamefully averts his eyes and keeps walking. So many people wielding fire in their hands.

Suddenly a shout issues from a megaphone, an incomprehensible phrase, a Portuguese without vowels, and the line of police surges forward. With the National Theater behind them, the cops, brandishing their dark helmets and transparent shields, advance toward the protesters. Americo stops to watch. It's all very theatrical, actually. It is written, it must always go this way: someone makes an overly expressive gesture, a movement outside the choreographed standard, and, in the blink of an eye, there are billyclubs bludgeoning the heads of doctors, nurses, and aides; and stones being thrown, and stethoscopes used as weapons, and women with wedding rings and conventional hairdos biting the arms and legs of riot police; and burning banners and torn clothing and white smocks splattered with red; and bloodied noses, mouths, foreheads and eyes, and Americo doesn't even flinch. On the contrary, it has quite a healing effect. His heart is becalmed after such a spectacular show of force, so up-close. The life of others.

In the dream a man exactly like him awakens on the sofa in Murilo's living room, sits up and looks around in the usual desultory fashion, sighs idiotically and, finally, as if he were lugging thirty kilos of bitterness, disaffection, and failure, drags himself through the hallway looking for the bathroom. When he awakens, Americo more or less does the same.

In the bathroom, balanced on the faucet in the sink, there is a hastily scribbled note: *Americo, gotta go. Affairs of the heart heart heart dontcha know know know. Lunch at 2 at Galeto? See yamigo, Murilo.*

There is an unmistakably feminine touch in all this. The notion of a note, the paper on the sink, the brevity, the *heart heart heart* without commas. It is not an image that buoys him: Murilo and some chick running to the bathroom in fits of laughter while he snores open-mouthed on the living room sofa. Who can it be this time? Some martial arts expert, a moneyed foreigner, the daughter of an old girlfriend? Americo, surly from sleep, pictures them traipsing through gardens, taking in terraces, skating around Lisbon gorging on the pastries in Belém and drowning in *ginjinha* and fruit juice. And, during the pauses in their romantic idyll, commenting on, to the point of tedium, the pathetic figure on the sofa, replaying the scene and laughing until they cried. This actor of respectable renown, who has played some of the most important roles in the repertoire of international theater, who has worked with some of the most esteemed directors (from Portugal and abroad), and who has even acted in a primetime soap opera (albeit in a supporting role, but one crucial to the development of the central storyline), lying there on the couch, mouth agape, armpits stinking and nose bent upwards, and producing an unthinkable snore of catastrophic and unprecedented intensity, what a joke. In the shower, beneath the absurdist dribble of water that's either too hot or too cold, Americo screeches with rage.

Back in the front room, he opens to a random passage from Bernardo Soares: *To read is to dream by the hand of another. To misread is to free ourselves from the hand that guides us.* He opens to a random passage from Simone Weil: *Hunger is a relation to food surely much less complete but as real as the act of eating.* He opens to a random passage from Groucho Marx: *Love is undoubtedly responsible for the baby boom, but even love (as powerful as it is) requires the presence of the stronger sex, and the stronger sex, during this period, was way too busy opening up new trade routes.*

At lunch with Murilo—a quick snack at the bar that turns out to be more professional than personal—the takeaway comes down to these five things. One: Americo must get himself a lawyer right away. Two: Murilo cannot be the one to represent him because, aside from the fact that his life is in a state of "cosmic chaos," he doesn't like to work (much less pro bono), is not a specialist in family law, in fact, has so little patience for laws, legal proceedings, deadlines, courts, etc., that, as his client, Americo would risk being robbed, ridiculed, and even deported to some horrid and far-flung country from which an obscure ancestor might have once emigrated. Three: Murilo already knows the perfect lawyer, a fierce, knowledgeable man, exactly the type that Americo needs, a classmate of Murilo's from law school, one of the best students, the kind with a super-high GPA but not one of those total geeks, not one of those theoretical nerds that are always lousy comrades in the clinch. Four: Americo has to start showing a "serious interest" in his son, try to see him whenever he can, buy him diapers and toys on a regular basis, get him a savings account, and keep all statements and receipts so that later Joana's lawyer doesn't use the lack of this against him, and he must also make an exhaustive list of every little screwup that his future ex-wife made concerning the care of their son when they "shared a common household," things like coming home late for dinner or rushing out to work in the morning and leaving the father Americo to tend to the poos and the pees and the feedings and the screams. And five: he mustn't get depressed or succumb to the temptation for resignation, lamentation or self-pity himself (it's curious how, every now and then, his bohemian friend comes out with such harsh, almost Biblical utterances). He must, instead, rejoice and celebrate (but, please, far from the public eye). Now he is a new man, a free man, and freedom is the best thing there is.

He leaves Galeto and it is as if he has entered the subtle shade of a nightmare. On the surface, nothing has changed; the scene is the same as always—the city, the blue sky. But, underneath, behind everything—the cars, the trees, the trash cans, the billboards—something lurks. Something is watching him. It's nothing he can see, but he can feel it, yes, he knows it's there. A presence, a fear. He doubles around to the restaurant to get himself a shot of old liquor to fortify himself against these stupid phantoms, and he sees the huge red letter *M*, hovering like an apparition over the Metro station. He runs for the staircase, buys a ticket in the machine and flees, without waiting for his change.

He takes the subway to the end of the line. He doesn't want to go anywhere; he just wants to *be* somewhere. Somehow, the monotonous, metallic, mechanical hum of the moving train has a soothing effect on his nerves.

Seated at the far end of the subway car—very discreetly, without making a fuss—he expels as much air as he can.

Outside it is completely dark. What would Paul Giamatti do in his position?

And so, acting in allegiance to his character, Americo ends up in a stuffy and crowded shopping mall and, to the accompaniment of syrupy violin music and sighs of "I love you," searches for some gifts for Joachim. A toy car with working headlights and real engine noises. A stuffed anti-allergenic bunny. A giant pack of extra-small Ultra-Comfort diapers.

He arrives at Murilo's house late in the afternoon, dead tired, wielding a perfectly obscene amount of brightly colored shopping bags. Murilo is slicing up a pink onion in the kitchen. With tears in his eyes, he asks Americo how his day went. "It went well, can't you see?" says Americo, setting down the shopping bags. "And thanks, man."

"For what?"

"For all this ... this support."

"Oh, it's nothing. The least I can do. That's what friends are for, right? Times like these, no?"

"Well, you don't have to cry about it ...."

Murilo bursts out laughing.

Americo picks up the bags. "I'll put these away and be back."

"By any chance, could you dine out tonight?"

"Tonight?" Americo repeats, as if he's never heard the word.

"I am preparing a romantic dinner for Juraya and ...."

"Oh."

"So, you don't mind?"

"No," says Americo. "No, of course not," he says, sensing that his words are not quite in sync with his lips. "Sure, I don't mind at all."

At the Viseense Café, he gets lucky and finds a seat facing the television. There's a debate on between the Prime Minister and the leader of the opposition about the "state of the nation," under the pretext of the recent demonstrations in the major cities, the topic being "the widespread climate of instability," the "disenchantment of the professional classes," and the "grave social crisis affecting larger and larger segments of the population." Inside a blue studio, two men in suits and ties and a woman in a yellow dress are seated between red rectangular desks that are much too large for them. Play-Doh politics. The woman, of course, is the journalist. She smiles to her right, she smiles to her left. The two politicians look at her fearlessly; they smile back at her but in a much more restrained fashion (and the one on the left even more restrained than the one on the right). Americo eats grilled grouper with potatoes and broccoli and lots of olive oil.

Watching the screen, he follows their gestures, their expressions, their glances, concentrates on details like the color of their neckties, their style of jacket, the model of their eyeglasses. With nothing better to do, he even tries to follow the discussion about "diverse societal models"—if he understands it correctly, one wants fewer poor people and the other wants more rich people—but at a certain point a child wanders into the blue studio and this breaks his concentration. A child, right in the middle of a live television show. A small child, who they let climb up on the desks and crawl all over the place. The gentlemen continue speaking as if nothing has happened—"because I this," "because I that"—while the journalist seems a bit thrown by the whole scene but attempts to disguise it—"because the average citizen at home is seeking clear answers"—and no one does a thing about, shall we say, the elephant in the room. As if it were possible that any viewer hasn't noticed a child running loose in the middle of a televised political debate. The Prime Minister says, "Your numbers are all wrong," and the leader of the opposition says, "Do not interrupt me, sir," and the child turns to the camera (*This will not end well*, thinks Americo, looking around to see if anyone in the restaurant has seen it. *This will end badly for sure*) and babbles: "Ma-ma!"

It's his son. My God, it's Joachim.

Lifting a forkful of broccoli to his mouth, Americo is pounded by a gigantic wave of grief. A terrible wave, rising from within, a grief as powerful as if the little shit had died or something. As if his beloved son (God forbid) had died and gone to a better place. And suddenly, everything is folded into everything else—the television, the politics, the restaurant, his life, all jumbled together with the flavor of a classic legume, one with the consistency of broccoli—at once hard, soft, and somewhere in between, and covering his mouth with his hand to avoid yet more indelicacies, Americo lets loose the greatest public belch of his thirty-five years on Earth.

Saturday, at ten in the morning, he is in front of No. 81, loaded down with bags and with the same butterflies as someone about to go on stage. The day before he had phoned Joana to see if he could pass by for a visit, but the high-level bureaucrat wasn't exactly thrilled with the notion. "Oh what now?" she screamed into the phone. She didn't even bother to ask where he was, whether or not he was doing okay, if he was suicidal or simply suffering his usual poetic melancholy. Americo thought it best not to reveal too much. If she's not interested, I won't be the one to play the sad sack. He simply added, with utmost delicacy, in his sweetest voice, that he missed them like crazy, that these had been the most difficult days of his life, that he would never betray her, not her nor anyone else, ever, ever again. He even embellished it further, like one of those cheeseball actors, by padding it with another chorus of "ever, ever, ever again." He actually said "ever" three times. Christ, what a horror. He told her that now he truly valued what they had "built together, the three of them," and that a life alone was meaningless. And, as he said this, he sobbed, just a little, so his wife would see that he really meant it.

"So, listen," she said, interrupting him mid-sob. "What exactly do you want to come here for?"

He almost hung up the phone. What a travesty, having to ask for permission to go to one's own house. "I just need to fetch a few things … some books and papers, work stuff. For the movie I'm doing and the plays I'm … thinking, the, uh, projects, I'm, you know, developing."

Silence on the other end.

"And also to see the two of you, of course. Joachim and you …."
More silence.

He couldn't think of anything else to say. "Joana?" The pause lasted so long he began to think that perhaps there was no one on the other line, that the telephone from which his voice issued, the receiver through which he was so thoroughly humiliating himself, stammering sentimentalities, sobbing like a moron, perhaps had been dropped in a corner somewhere, forgotten on the sofa or on that squat little table made out of a tree-trunk with the plastic ashtray where he and his wife used to leave all those things they didn't know what to do with—paper clips, rubber bands, those little copper one-, two-, and five-cent coins. "Joana, are you there?" How ridiculous—in the largest room in the house, a rectangular room almost three meters high, in that immense void, speaking in vain, unnecessarily humiliating himself in a meek little voice, "Please … are you there?"

And then she said: "Be here tomorrow at ten." That tone, that particular little tone of hers, the same curt tone that she uses to dispatch telemarketers. Cruel, so cruel, my God, why is this world so damned cruel?

Americo sets down the shopping bags. He takes a deep breath, combs what little hair he has left. He picks up the bags. He rings the doorbell.

When Daddy flies him around in circles like a tiny plane in the amusement park, Joachim roars with laughter. The world seen from above, spinning fast, faster. Americo laughs as well, sensing his eyes filling with a heavy moisture.

"Everything all right?" asks Joana.

"Everything, sure," says Americo, putting down his son. "I've brought some surprises."

Quickly, so that the moment doesn't set off another alarm in his fragile, emotional heart, he pulls the gifts from the bag (all of the receipts he's kept, yes) and offers them to the boy and his mother with a strained smile: "I didn't quite know what to bring …."

"And so you brought the whole store."

While Joachim amuses himself with the packages, Americo dashes off to what used to be his "little nook and cranny," grabs his computer, the screenplay for *Being Paul Giamatti*, and half a dozen books. He stuffs as many clothes as he can rescue from the drawers into a suitcase—unpaired socks, old boxer shorts.

"Say bye-bye to Daddy. Come on, Joachim say good-bye …."

He kisses his son good-bye and shakes his wife's hand, then vanishes in a flash. He hates farewells.

He drags the suitcase—*kok, pok, zok*—through the streets of old Lisbon. The world, damn it, has become an unfathomable place. Where did these narrow, twisted streets come from, so unwieldy, so perfectly illogical?

When he gets to the corner, a little man in a black coat and a pompadour appears out of thin air. He looks like he's stepped out of a late Sunday afternoon from the 1980s. "Mr. Abril, the actor?" he asks. There is an innocent expression on his face.

10. Simulacrum and Shadow

There are two of them, actually. Behind the short one with the pompadour, there's an even weirder-looking guy with a shaved head and gray eyes, a kind of plainclothes pharaoh. But it's the pompadour who does the talking. He says his name is Rosado, inspector for the Federal Police. He flashes some kind of ID from his pocket that Americo barely sees, proceeds to explain that they are not there "in an official capacity" and asks if Americo could accompany them. "We'd just like to have a couple words with you."

Before Americo can say that, as a matter of fact, this isn't the best time, Rosado grabs his suitcase and proceeds down the street. "Let me help you with this."

"You don't need …."

"You know what we want to discuss with you, do you not?"

"As a matter of fact, no—"

"We are investigating the murder of a woman, Carla Bruna, an employee of Club Erox, who was involved with … let's say she cultivated some complex relationships, and we'd like you to help us understand, in any way you can, some of these aspects a little better. Purely …." Then, as if struck by another thought, the inspector turns back to the pharaoh with the strange eyes. "Forgive me, I forgot to introduce the two of you."

"What?" Americo says.

"This is my colleague, Nogueira. Nogueira, say hello to the gentleman."

The man regards Americo with funereal seriousness. "Hello."

"Anyway, as I was saying," Rosada continues, picking up his stride, "we are here on a purely informal basis. 'Unofficial,' if you prefer. Understood?"

Americo has no clue where all this is heading. "Yes, I think so …."

"Very well, then. First off, how were you related to the victim?"

"What?"

"Not what—*how?*"

"How?"

"With Carla Bruna, how were you related to her?"

"I was related by … related by … we were lovers."

"'Lovers'?"

"Exactly."

"I can, therefore, deduce from your words that the relationship was of a sexual nature?"

Americo pauses. Sexual nature? Christ, he'd rather be anywhere else than here. He glances back and pictures himself fleeing down the street to somewhere far, far away. But on second thought, no, he'd better not. Something about Nogueira's frozen expression dissuades him. "Yes," he says. "Yes … it was."

"Did you pay her?"

"No, no I did not."

He is quite nervous but aside from that (or perhaps the two things are somehow connected), he can't help but feel a certain sense of farce about accompanying these two goons through the crosswalk. The absurd spectacle of a police inspector dragging his suitcase full of flattened clothing down the streets of Lisbon.

"So, you're telling us that she actually *liked* you, is that it?" says Nogueira.

Americo responds with a laugh.

"So then," says Rosado, "did you pay her or not?"

"Yes. I mean, no. I didn't pay her for ... that. There was no ... she never .... No, I, well, sometimes ... left her some ... gifts. For ... well, because I, um, liked her. Understand? Get it?"

"Sometimes?"

"Almost always. Always ... perhaps."

"What kind of 'gifts'?"

Nogueira, upon hearing this, laughs a theatrical, inopportune laugh. Amused, Rosado looks back at him. Americo attempts to laugh along with them, hoping it will defuse the moment, but the police, now grim as plaster statues, stop themselves, and wait for him to say the word. The ugliest, most obscene word of all.

Americo averts his eyes. An irredeemable pile of dog shit steams on the sidewalk. "Money," he says. "Some banknotes under the lamp ...."

A few meters ahead, the inspectors get in an old white Opel Corsa parked on the sidewalk and speed off. Nobody notices. Americo looks around; people pass by, preoccupied with their own little lives, heads down, hands in their pockets, laughing into their cell phones.

He sits on top of his suitcase, not knowing where to go. What the fuck just happened? The two goons, the "unofficial chat," the strange looks, what could it all possibly mean? He gets up, grabs the handle of the suitcase, but he doesn't move. The street rises steeply up to a slithering sky. Were they really cops? Did that really just happen? Is any of this really happening? Stricken with panic, Americo takes off running down the street.

He heads towards Murilo's house but before he reaches the end of the street he changes his mind. He senses that someone is following him. Behind the noise—*kok, pok, zok*—of the suitcase, Americo perceives the sound of footsteps. Not the typical sound of someone walking down the street, but a more circumspect, conscious, less spontaneous—a *deliberate* sound, my God. To calm his nerves, he counts to ten with long, deep breaths in between and, when he gets to ten, he turns and enters the first open door he sees.

"Good morning," says a young woman behind an empty counter. Her hair is in braids; she has red lips and long lashes.

"Good morning."

"Let me know if I can be of any assistance."

"Um, yes. OK. Thank you very much."

Magazines hang on the walls. Rusty nails, hammered asymmetrically into the stucco, hold in place cheap strings that, in turn, hold in place fake magazines.

The visitor to the gallery is thusly invited to participate in the artist's project through a simple action: the common, everyday, humdrum action of picking out a magazine here gains a new dynamic. A dynamic, shall we say, complicit in its own risk and dramatic potential. And, this is only by virtue of an empirical dislocation, an injection of meaning attained through the medium of a subtle change of context, of environment, thus introducing—by an application which, in relation to the fulcrum of artistic intention that this sculpture-painting-installation-performance art, is, we should stress, actually marginal *or* secondary, *or, to state it another way, secondary in the sense of marginal and not in the sense of less relevant—to the core of the piece a commentary on urban space/spaces, the public/private duality, the solemn/sacred/ sanctified nature of the artistic work versus the disposable/recyclable/ relative nature of contemporary existence (or, at the very least, of its metaphorical echo in the field of ideas, which some might classify as, perhaps, the essence of time), etc. Beyond this, these objects-magazines with colors that spill from one page to the next, disregarding the very notion of the "page"; painted magazines, yes, but filled with phrases which, at the far reaches of legibility, redeem such realms as classic poetry, the philosophical avant-garde, and the theological void, thus subverting the conventional, prosaic chrome-pop culture; thus piercing, fearlessly and heedlessly, our preconceived image of what is or isn't a magazine; magazines that toy with the very notion of the name "maga-zine," that call themselves a "gazette" or a "periodical" or a "journal" or an "issue" or a "digest" or a "review," as if all things needed to be "re-viewed" or "re-seen" because what is lacking, what we all lack as individuals and as a community, is a return to our inception, to what is, at once, the most fundamental and the most onerous, because what we lack, precisely, is this, and only this, the relearning of how to see, that is, to re-see, to re-view—these objects possess, as well, a unitary, sui generis worth, transformed unto themselves by a beauty that, at once, fractures and redeems, disassembles and illuminates, obfuscates and immortalizes them; that, in the end, bolsters them like the most sympathetic of the cheap strings from which they hang.*

Americo is attempting to decipher the tortured phrases on the corner of the magazine page when he realizes that the woman with the braids is standing behind him, trying to catch a peek at what he's reading. "It's okay to touch?"

"Of course," she says. "Sorry, but I couldn't resist. It's just that I … it happens that … well, I shouldn't be telling you this, but … I'm the one who did this."

"The magazines?"

"I call them *Magazine* in the singular. As if it were always the one thing, get it?"

"Yes. Yes, I do," he says, without getting a thing.

"As if it were always the one magazine and these were some of the issues from that single magazine."

"It's … interesting."

The woman lets loose a little giggle and bites on her right braid. "Where are you off to?" she asks suddenly, looking at the suitcase that Americo pulls behind him like a squashed shadow.

"Ah, no. I'm not …. I'm only going to a friend's house and …."

"Forgive me; it's none of my business."

"No, it's fine, I'm just going to visit a friend. Just for a couple days."

The woman puts the braid back in her mouth.

Without speaking, Americo retreats into the magazine he holds in his hands, slowly turning the pages. He exaggerates the time that he spends looking at each image as one is supposed to do when looking at "art."

"I thought you were going to say some city or country."

"What?"

"When I asked you about your suitcase. I like to guess about people, where they go. Sometimes I get it right. When someone says, for example, 'Amsterdam.' Or better yet, 'Sao Vincente.' Sometimes I get it right off, nail it perfectly, match exactly the face of the person with the city they tell me. Understand?"

"No, as a matter of fact I don't!"

They share a laugh.

"Or countries," she says. "It works well with countries too."

"Countries?"

"Yes. Sierra Leone. Surinam."

"Scotland? Taiwan?"

"Mongolia."

"Malaysia."

"The United States of America."

"The United States, are you certain? Yes, perhaps. May I treat *mademoiselle* to it, then?"

"But of course."

"But *mademoiselle* is obliged to reciprocate, *oui*?"

"Oh, yes?" she says. Her eyelashes glisten with mascara; her smile is ambiguous. "But it has to be just *America*."

"How's that?"

"For it to work, it has to be just *America*. Not *The United States of America*, unabbreviated. Don't you think?"

"For me, yes, that would be better," he says, stretching out his hand. "Because my name is … *Americo*. Americo Abril."

The woman clasps his hand. "Victoria."

The artist takes him on a guided tour through the "secret parts" of the gallery, which she likes to call "our true stage set."

"Kind of your 'backstage'?" asks Americo.

"Yes, more or less. Over there's the kitchen. And here is our little sound studio."

"Lots of stuff …."

"And behind this door," she says, with a wink, "is the 'Area of Practical Matters.'"

As she says this, the door opens, behind which appears a huge dark-skinned man with dark glasses and shoulder-length hair. Victoria introduces them.

"Juan Miriades, Americo Abril."

"Nice to meet you," Americo says, shaking his monstrous Spanish hand.

Juan says nothing. He flashes a tired smile, like that of a superstar on tour.

"Working much?" asks the actor, pointing to the office.

But the giant pretends not to understand. He pulls a chocolate bar out of his pocket, breaks off a square, and offers it to Americo.

Americo holds the square gingerly between the tips of his fingers, as if it were a rare jewel or a highly delicate explosive. "*Gracias*," he says, in his best Spanish.

But Juan only has eyes for Victoria: "*Quieres?*"

"Not right now," says the artist, and the two of them head toward a red door.

Americo looks at the square of chocolate, sticks it in his mouth. It's chocolate on the outside, something else inside. A chewy filling with an unexpected taste, not entirely disagreeable. Leaves? Flowers?

"Coming?" Victoria asks.

Americo shakes his head. He needs to return to the world, get some air, clear his head.

"Come on," she says. "Let me show you the upstairs, then you can go."

———

He awakens on a dirty sofa, in a dark room, with the taste of cloth in his mouth. He has no idea where he is or what's happened. "Victoria?" He gets up to open the curtain. It's dark red, heavy, in the grand style of the theater, and much too big for the window.

It's night outside; the streets are deserted.

Americo presses his nose to the window. He doesn't understand how he got here. How long have I been sleeping? And where, exactly, am I? He looks around. It must have been that square of chocolate. Something illegal, no doubt. "Victoria?"

No one answers.

Walking down a long corridor with doors shut on either side, he begins to hear a racket. A strong, steady beat, mixed with the sounds of human voices, shouts, cries. Suddenly, the light goes out. Americo leans hard against the wall. He waits a few seconds, breathing deeply. Someone else, close by, seems to be breathing along with him. Is it human? Or animal?

He crouches down, his hands in the air, the pathetic figure of a man afraid of everything—when the lights come on, he is in a room filled with women in bikinis, who burst into spontaneous applause.

"My dear Americo!" says Victoria, stepping out between two of the voluptuous forty-somethings with the regal bearing of a lion-hunter. She is the only woman completely dressed, which grants her a certain authority over the rest of the group. "Do you see what we have prepared for you?" she asks, stretching out her arms and gesturing toward the half-naked multitude.

He tries to laugh, but all he can manage is a forced grimace.

Fortunately someone pushes a button and the music begins. The women leap and shout and dance, their mouths agape with joy. While Victoria steers him toward a corner with a makeshift bar, Americo notices clusters of foam spewing from tubes suspended from the ceiling. The lights dim; colors and images are cast against the bodies, against the walls, against everything.

"Are you all right?"

"Yes, of course …," says Americo. "Stick by me, okay?"

Victoria smiles and turns her back, then disappears into the crowd of dancing women. Americo, taking it all in, doesn't know whether to thank her or not. The music pumps and pounds, arms and legs disappear and reappear out of a large cloud of foam. Nothing about any of this seems like a "true stage set."

Leaning against the bar, Americo drinks a glass of Douro and, savoring its fruity notes, the hints of oak, the nuances achievable only through the semi-artisanal process of a long family history in the region, he thinks how nice it is to be inside such a "work of art"— and, feeling a warmth masquerading as an inner peace, he imagines that, in the final analysis, his life is nothing but a grand, way-over-the-top performance, that Carla Bruna isn't really dead, that Joana doesn't really hate him, that he is not really doomed to share just a few crumbs of his son's future, no, it's all just a sham, a joke, nothing but, to borrow a phrase that some art critic wrote in the catalog for the exhibit of the hanging magazines, "simulacrum and shadow," all just a kind of "installation-in-progress," and one of these days he'll wake up and, finally getting the joke, he'll magnanimously applaud the great deception.

"Where do I sign up?" Murilo asks the next morning, when Americo recounts his surreal experience in the Gallery of Victoria With the Braids. "Hyper-realist, you called it? Or was it postmodernist? Um … can you tell me about those bikinis again?"

Americo is sitting in his friend's kitchen, eating "a blend of cereal flakes designed to bring quality of life to your digestive system." Murilo, arms folded across his chest, stands and looks at him. He doesn't have the usual shrunken expression; in fact it's quite the opposite: there's something almost maternal in the way he waits for his friend to finish his cereal. "Do you want a smoothie?"

Americo looks up at the lawyer's weasely countenance. The smile is too generous, the expression constricted; there is guiltiness stashed away somewhere. "You want me to leave, right?"

"Sorry, man, it's just that Luciana Maria is on her way and it would probably be best if ... you don't mind ..., if you could ...."

"Of course," he says. "It's all good. No problem."

He is stepping off the elevator, dragging his sad little suitcase on wheels behind him—*kok, pok, zok*—when he sees her entering the building. She walks towards him as if in slow motion, her head tilting slightly to the left, slightly to the right, pretending not to notice him, standing directly in front of her, deeply immersed in the role of the chivalrous gentleman, holding the door open for her to pass through. Luciana Maria. No older than eighteen, rail-thin, tall as a giraffe, Modiglianian neck, legs for days. Spiderlike, cool as a cucumber. Where does Murilo find these babes?

"Good morning."

"Thank you," says the girl, as she disappears into the elevator.

Americo releases the door with a sigh and recalls some old verses, *Some eyes bring envy / they're blue and they're worthless / some eyes bring heartache / they're black and they're mirthless ....*

The moment he steps onto the street, a baby-faced journalist thrusts a microphone in his face, "Americo Abril? Would you care to comment on the accusations linking you to the Case of The Bod?"

"What?" says Americo, and takes off running.

But the bastard is persistent, sticks close behind him on the sidewalk, brandishing the recorder over his shoulder, in front of his mouth, trying to catch any sound, the slightest hesitation, any trivial little hiccup that might implicate the actor right into the society pages of tomorrow's edition.

"Any comments on the ongoing investigation? Do you have confidence in the Portuguese justice system? Have you been contacted by anyone connected to the case?"

"Please," he says, stopping at the corner. He thrusts his arm out tautly in front of him, like a basketball player protecting an imaginary ball.

The journalist is either stupidly serene or bored to death. He looks at Americo, then at the recorder, then back at Americo.

"Thank you very much," says the actor.

But the journalist doesn't even blink. He wears the glazed, insipid look of the certified moron. "Can you confirm that your marriage to Joana de Miranda Rosas has been compromised by this crisis? I'm referring to the recent publicity about the case of the death of Carla Bruna, the 'Luxury Lady of the Lisboan Evening,' also known as 'The Bod' or 'The Object' .... No? Nothing? Any comment at all, Mr. Americo Abril? And the theater? Do you intend to continue performing after this scandal?"

A sudden heat rises to his head; in a fraction of a second, his entire life, from A to Z, like in some idiotic summer rerun—unloosed, unfiltered images—streams past at the speed of thought; he and his mother in an overly proper living room, he and his father in a five-star asylum, he and his son, the baby gangster, on a Lisbon boulevard, he and his frigid wife in a marriage bed, he and his dead mistress in a hotel room (this only 75 percent imaginary), he and his character in the American movie traversing an airport lobby bathed in a singular, incredible, exuberant, soul-stirring light—and the actor—*pow!*—punches the journalist right in the kisser.

The young fellow falls backward, losing his balance, an irrevocable jackass. Americo watches him fall, watches him grope on the pavement for the tape recorder or a loose battery or a loose tooth. His eyes are red; they betray more fear than suffering. The actor pivots, grabs a cab, splits, *See ya.*

It is only when he's inside the taxi that he sees, framed by the rear window, as if in a photograph, another guy, his colleague. He's got a camera instead of eyes, and the eye of that camera is staring right at him. Fucking photographer.

"Where to?"

The jagged head of the cabbie disrupts his thoughts. For a brief instant, Americo doesn't know what to say. "Uhh ... go ... just ... keep going, please."

"Keep going?"

Through the windows of the taxi the facades spin and twist and recede, and the city, gorging with monstrous billboards, clothes hanging in windows, torn posters, walls mottled with graffiti, the everyday city gradually becomes an abstraction, transforming into blocks of pallid colors, surfaces devoid of context, immense changes taking hold with every turn of the steering wall, only much more slowly. In the back seat of the cab, a strange odor infuses itself into Americo's senses, and suddenly he's a little boy, in the midst of summer, standing on a plastic chair in the back yard of his house. His father is turning the page of his newspaper and his mother is coming out the house with a big jar of lemonade. "Americo, don't stand up on the chair," "What? What? What?," "It was made with our very own lemons, let's see how it tastes," "Here comes the IMF, now we're all in their pocket," and he considers whether or not to jump, a superman flying over the yard. The smell of the earth beneath the freshly cut grass. The odor of lemons with his face pressed against the lip of the jar. "Americo, that's disgusting." His mother's aroma beneath her perfume. "What? What?" The rustle of paper, of hands folding the newspaper, the odor of the thick pages, of newsprint, his father's intense bearing, the pungent aroma of wisdom that issued from all those answers to all his questions. "What?"

"This is fine, here. Pull over to the right, please."

Wedged between a police parking lot and the highway, the massive three-star hotel is a monument to solitude. A reasonably priced room, slathered in red and beige; a painting of horses on the wall. Through the window, in the distance, the black skeleton of the viaduct. Americo plugs his cell phone into its charger and lies down to read the book he packed in his suitcase. *The Married Woman.* A so-called "adult novel" he lifted from Murilo's house. He reads the first chapter, where he's introduced to a "corpulent young beauty in white" and "a most sophisticated crime." Then he calls Joana.

He tries four times. He pictures his family at home as if it were another family in another house, with the phone ringing so loudly that the place itself grows larger and more violent. He pictures Joana in the living room waiting for the ringing to cease, so furious that she doesn't even move. You can't even pick up the phone? Answer the goddamn telephone.

He nods off when he gets to chapter five, right after the protagonist, a Swedish-African woman who "runs errands" for the MI5, has seduced an old arms dealer in a Russian yacht anchored in international waters teeming with sinister white sharks and listless hammerheads. He turns on his side and has a dream for the ages.

A red phone rings underwater. It's one of those old-style phones, very '80s, set into the hollow recess of a boulder, amongst waving algae and dancing shadows. Americo, who in the dream is fast asleep, is awakened by the ringing and dives from the hotel room into the sea to pick it up. He knows that from that phone, out of that retro receiver, some fundamental word will issue forth. A mystery, the revelation of some mystery. A solution, perhaps, to the unstable situation in the floating room.

But when he lifts the receiver to his ear, he hears only bubbles. Air bubbles, as if someone were breathing into the telephone. Bubbles that don't burst—on the contrary, they keep swelling, and rising, ceaselessly, to the surface. And swelling, expanding even afterwards, surging out of the water and piercing through the foam and floating up to the blue sky which, in Americo's dream, is a sort of upside-down well, without a bottom.

11. February 29

"At three in the afternoon, the first people began to arrive and within a few minutes there was all this commotion at the foot of the Assembly staircase," explains the man in the pink shirt and straw hat, clutching a *No Standing or Parking* sign with the desperation of a drowning man pulled down by the undertow. Americo nods.

The immensity of it all. The fact is that no one knows what's going on, nobody knows for certain from where all this comes. The strong, silent masses, with no core, no leader, no voice, no goal, yet focused, tense, expectant. People in incongruous clothing—dark suits, colorful scarves, unfashionable hats—gathering in slipshod fashion. It is said that the call for the gathering was spread by text. It is said that it was circulated through the Internet, through the miracle of social media. It is said that there are semi-covert organizations, obscure movements made up of contradictory interests, that, in one form or another—with money, contacts, or ideas—have contributed to the success of the "Happening." If you can call it that, considering nothing has yet happened. And it's not exactly a "demonstration" either. Everyone looks towards one another, waiting for who knows what, but as yet there is no collective declaration, no disavowal or demand, no rebuff or request. No one is protesting anything. It's all quite odd. Nowhere, amidst this mass of diversity gathered all in one place, is there a *What?* to be heard. Only, perhaps, a reflective *What now*? Or, perhaps, from the forest primeval, an instinctive *What if*? All these people—young, old, men, women—so tightly pressed together, so thrilled to be here. So fucking weird.

"Yeah, it was all word-of-mouth," says a blue-eyed girl in a ponytail. "One by one, eye to eye, mouth to mouth." And, all around her, everyone laughs, except Americo.

There are many versions, but the truth is that no one knows for certain how all this began, what it was that gave birth to such a multitude. An immense body that seems to have sprung out of nowhere, filling up São Bento Square, and that now overflows into the adjacent streets, spreading uptown toward Estrela and downtown to Poço dos Negros. Actual places overrun by an inconceivable public, über-real people made up of Nature's intrinsic incongruity. Actual, living people who don't show up in statistics, who don't respond to opinion polls, who defy the data of market researchers. An old man in a white suit with a kid on his back, invoking the names of soccer stars. A girl with a book in one hand and a baseball bat in the other. A woman with coiffed hair embracing a man with a sliced earlobe. No doubt some have stumbled upon all this by pure chance. Like himself, for instance, who just happened to be passing by after lunch with Andrade-Pinto at a chic restaurant in Santos. They devoured the degustation menu while bellyaching about life, kids, aging, money, the nation, the "system." He's becoming a bore, thought Americo, as he fled the scene. And doubtless Andrade-Pinto was thinking the very same thing about him.

The truth is that, since the death of Carla Bruna or since Joana booted him out of the house, he's felt this way. He's become tiresome to himself.

He can't recall this ever happening before. In fact he's almost certain it hasn't. On the contrary, he even used to arrange it so he had free time, just for himself, often using work as an excuse, under the pretense that he needed to study a particular role, to isolate himself so he could "get into character," when what he really wanted was some "alone time." Yes, before all this went down—the death, the separation—he actually quite enjoyed his own company. Now everything has become so banal, so flat, so static, so superficial. So lifeless ....

Just then, a voice. Americo lifts his head. This could be the title of one of those runaway bestsellers: *A Voice in the Crowd*. He can tell from what vicinity the words are coming from, but he cannot see the speaker's face. A short person, a woman, perhaps, although the voice is rather deep, gruff almost, an instrument through which much air is squandered, through which much breath issues forth without a note being played, or just barely grazes one or two intelligible syllables. This voice now rises above the heads of the crowd. Americo stops to listen. He can't quite make out complete sentences, only a word or two that lingers, hovering low over the hairdos, the hairless, the hats. Unloosed words: *Today, we, question.* Or is it *questing*?

It's not much, but it's enough. And just when the voice falls silent the crowds begin to move toward the stone steps. The famous national staircase. They do not run; there is no sign of euphoria or panic. They move at a slow, steady pace, all at once, without hesitation, as if they've known from the beginning it would be like this, that it could only be like this.

The police stand and watch. Vests, shields, billy clubs, at the ready. Except for the eyes. It's quite apparent that the poor souls don't know what to do about all this; this Happening (yes, now something is *happening*), this multitude advancing in response to the mysterious question of the mysterious woman. A mob that doesn't move in the usual way, that doesn't "advance" in the proper sense, but glides forward as if propelled, by its own weight, toward the first step on the staircase of the Legislature. People, arms at their sides, packed in together like in the Metro at rush hour, yet still rolling forward. And the silence of a thousand bodies, breathing as one.

The faces of the police, dear God, what an ineffable scene: eyes bulging behind their visors, teeth biting on their lips. It's clear as day: everything is hanging by a thread. The poor cops will panic, will take out their billy clubs, their rubber-bullet guns, the fire hoses, the tear gas grenades. This will be a bloodbath.

Americo is in the middle of the crowd, some twenty or thirty meters from the front lines. He can smell the odor of agriculture, of baby shampoo. He notices a policeman taking an order from a gadget tucked in his ear (the customary choreography of the attentive G-man: he lifts his hand to the ear, swivels to reveal his profile, Egyptian-like), and communicates an order to his colleagues manning the police line. In a flash they are backed up the staircase toward the entrance to the Assembly.

Dumbfounded by this initial triumph, the crowd stops in its tracks. Such ease is disconcerting. Are they awaiting reinforcements? But the doubts don't last long. The crowd soon begins pushing upward. The first skip up the stairs and turn back laughing like naughty schoolchildren; the rest ascend with the spare gestures of adults lost in thought. In less time than it takes to say "February twenty-ninth," the crowd has arrived at the headquarters of the Democracy.

Two-and-a-half hours later, they are all still at its door, awaiting who knows what. For the gates to open, for the deputies inside to get hungry, for the police outside to defect? There are no signs of fatigue on the part of the multitude. Some stand, others sit; some drink red wine, others eat ice cream. A beachlike atmosphere pervades the stone staircase; it's like a gigantic picnic. Leaning against a column, a young man with a thin Latino mustache plays a guitar and sings about "natural love in the cultural arena." A group of boys and girls who seem to know the song laugh loudly along with the lyrics and stand applauding. "Thank you very much," says the singer. Then he turns toward other folks, the silent majority who don't know him from Adam, and introduces himself. "Good afternoon, friends, I am Sandro the Unique, and it's a real pleasure to be here."

His second song is a ballad around the theme of staying put: "Dignity is to assent / all the rest is just lament, nobility is to stay afloat / all the rest is just revolt." Sandro sings, guitar in hand, stirring up the group of boys and girls: "Adventure is way overblown / the harder drug is stayin' home." At this point, as if to add musical potency to the lyrics, the song is suspended, at rest in an odd chord for two or three beats. And finally, the refrain: "Oh how lovely, oh how mellow / to be an old fart from Restelo," sings the young Sandro the Unique, at once dolorous and droll. Suddenly his fans get up on their feet, sing along with him, and clap their hands in time with the rhythm, "For love we die / For love we live / Love's really quite / conservative!"

And the crowd picks up the cue. It's an instinct, an unconscious response; a rustling of pure physical intelligence. The group of boys and girls stands up and, in a collective reflex, everyone around them stands up as well, Americo included, and eventually so do the thousands of people from there to Estrela and from there to Poço dos Negros, and then everyone advances at once against the great door of the Republic. The fans of Unique don't understand, exactly, what's going on, whether they should take the blame for all this or the credit, but also they don't much care; they just let themselves be swept along by the tide of people. Only the musician himself remains behind, seated and singing in the same spot, watching his left hand compose chords as if it had a will of its own.

There is nary a gesture, nor the minimal suggestion of violence. Only the weight of the Portuguese masses, arms slack, brave shoulders pressed against the constitutional portals. Nor even a harsh word—only a thousand, a million souls employing their weight in the most austere manner. Shoulders, foreheads, thighs, imagine.

Thus it begins.

Frightened by the reports they hear on the radio and on the Internet, the deputies decide to yield and order the police to open the doors. But the police refuse to obey. Technically, they do not receive their orders from the deputies, and don't report to the Parliament but to the Ministry of Internal Affairs. This is the version, at least, that reaches the street. A bit of news that, as such things go, soon appears in anecdotal form.

The deputies tell the police to open the doors: "This is an order, we are the representatives of the people!" And the police respond: "Fine, but have you heard the racket outside? The people are coming to dispatch their representatives!" And the deputies: "Oh, well it seems what we have here is judicial-political gridlock." And the police: "No profanity, please! We'll open the doors immediately!"

Thus it begins.

A magnificent chaos. Some of the deputies try to escape through the rear exits, through smaller, less "iconic" passageways; others take refuge in their offices. Others choose to take their places in the assembly chamber and, tightening their ties and retouching their eyeliner, fantasize about a glamorous martyrdom.

The people stream through the doors without fear or spectacle, with a guileless dignity. They, the people. They could not have achieved such a grand entrance had they rehearsed it for months. No one sobs, no one spits at the base of the columns. No one tells unsavory tales, nobody guffaws raucously, no one says a word. They all enter like kings, as if this had always been their home. Rendering this place, that looks so much bigger and uglier on television, into their palace. And they achieve this, all of it, with just a look. With a look and with the simple, disarming way they set foot on the floor of the assembly, their palace, their home. The way of *Yes*.

Thus, it begins.

12. Place of the Interior Arches

He is sitting on the ground, on a slope of the Douro River, thinking about nothing in particular, when two pairs of shoes appear before him. He counts to three before looking up. The shoes belong to two goons in suits. One is blond and chubby, the other dark-skinned and barrel-chested. They take off their sunglasses simultaneously, as if it were a dance routine.

"Good afternoon," says the blond one. "I'm Walser."

"Good afternoon," says the black one. "I'm Shulz."

They speak in English. Americo remains silent.

"Mr. Giamatti?" asks Walser.

Americo nods. Just once, so as not to look like a complete dolt.

"We are, what's the word, *representatives* of a well-known security company in the USA," says Shulz.

Walser looks over at his colleague. "Shulz is crazy about acronyms."

"We are here to i-n-t-e-r-r-o-g-a-t-e you."

"What, is this about that writer's microfilms?" asks Americo, forcing himself to look as nonchalant as possible.

Cut.

This is one of the key scenes of *Being Paul Giamatti*. Americo, the pseudo-Giamatti, has fled to Portugal, to Europe, and is staying in the house of a centenarian movie director who he met years ago at a masquerade ball in Venice. He believes he's inside a computer game called *Being Alive*. A game that ends either with his death or with his transformation into his true self, into the true Giamatti. But the truth is he can no longer be very certain about anything. In this scene, which, according to B. Kamp (the director), includes visual references to Chaplin, Rothko, Kitano, and Oliveira, the CIA agents, in the course of an investigation about a dangerous network of connections between the police and show business, come to interrogate him, but Giamatti mistakes them for "electronic phantoms" in the service of the Supergame, an annoyance that provokes a fit of rage. This misunderstanding of epic proportions takes a good half an hour to resolve.

"You must give us more!" B. Kamp shouts at him. "Open your eyes, try to be more … a little more … expressive, OK?"

Americo nods his head repeatedly. "Yes, yes …."

"Give it everything you've got, surrender yourself completely, bring it, damn it!"

"*Sim* … I mean, yes."

"Isn't it *alma* that you all say here? Isn't that what you're always saying in this country, to sing one's destiny and drink one's wine? So come on, put some *alma* into it, into your gestures, your lines, into that walrus body of yours, fuck!"

"Walrus?"

Five hours later the scene is done and Americo is dismissed for the day. "Don't stay out late tonight," warns the assistant director, a Scotsman named Hopston with hair down to his ass.

In order to exit the set, Americo has to pass through a gigantic red tube made of plastic, a translucent tunnel reminiscent of Euro Disney, Lego, sophisticated military operations in inhospitable places, and the NASA-quarantined house from that scene in E.T. with inflatable gangways to contain the "threat." It also resembles a monstrous umbilical cord. Americo treads carefully, a little freaked by the whole thing. All right maybe "freaked" is too strong a word;

perhaps "apprehensive" is more like it. "I believe they built this to make it easier to leave one's 'character,'" Vanessa Redgrave told him on the second day of shooting, a cigarette dangling from the corner of her mouth.

The tube leads him into the living room of the big granite house. On one side, an empty fireplace. On the other, a television facing a couch. Americo plops on the sofa, "Ahh ...." He feels nothing but an immense, bureaucratic fatigue.

On every channel they are broadcasting images of the crowds inside Parliament. After the building was occupied, on the 29th of February—a day that will be forever remembered as the Day of the New Revolution, the lucid hour when an untold number of citizens stormed in on their own feet, into the Assembly of the Republic, demanding nothing, following no savior of the fatherland, chanting not the customary cry of NO!, but instead an unprecedented, inquisitive and unforgettable YES—the idea emerged, born from that collective nebula from which tales, rumors, and legends spring, that each person would climb the steps, take his or her place at the Assembly rostrum, and propose a solution to a problem facing the country. Since then, every channel on every television station—public and private, network and cable—has broadcast nothing else.

A redheaded woman approaches the microphone and says we ought to pay more attention to city parks and gardens. A man in rolled-up sleeves says that the problem of public debt could be solved by printing new bills at the Mint or at the Bank of Portugal or wherever it is they print such things. A unkempt boy draws the audience's attention to the spiritual side of things. A woman on crutches says that we should have more children so the Portuguese people don't become extinct.

The next day Americo has another important scene to do: *The 2nd-Level Paul Giamatti Attempts to Reach the 3rd and Final Level!* To achieve this he must wrest the necessary info from the mega-powerful agent named Rodelius, who lives on a virtual island in the Douro River. This part of the script is written in a fast and loose style that combines the clichés of action movies with those of arthouse films. Nonetheless, there are moments of genuine brio ("Shakespearean, almost," quips Lady Redgrave), when, at the peak of the fight scene, the ghost of Giamatti the Elder, an old professor of literature and a renowned baseball theorist, materializes, exhorting his son to "Be more like your actual self." The ending is sad. Our man is trounced by Rodelius' cyborgs (they beat him to a bloody pulp and leave him upside-down in the cold waters of the river) and returns to the farm of the centenarian film director, bruised and battered, his soul verging on hypothermia.

"Still acting, are you?" Hopston asks.

Americo, quietly staring at his empty glass, doesn't know how to respond. The Scotsman isn't worth the effort. He's much too loaded and laughs at everything.

Every other evening there's a little informal party to celebrate the day's shooting. That is, an arrangement of colored streamers is hung over a table covered with bottles and glasses in the so-called "Mama's Room" of the manor house. Port, whiskey, moonshine, vodka. Tonight the mood is not exactly sanguine. Only Americo and Hopston, seated on the wood floor, defy the spirit, drinking and singing and blurting out whatever pops into their heads. Hopston tells a story about an actor who has a skiing accident and forgets everything—his name, his family, his country—everything he's ever read or imagined, and he can only recall certain lines from action movies, war films, Westerns, sci-fi flicks, and romantic comedies.

"Is this a crock or a true story?"

"And then ... he becomes President."

After the Scotsman goes off to bed ("It's a wrap ..."), Americo crawls to the couch, grabs the remote, and turns on the TV. He lies down and watches the parade of Lisboans, who, all day and all night, come rain or come shine, file up to that rostrum in the Assembly of the Republic. They adjust the thin microphone according to their height and speak the words they've pondered over or whatever inspires them at the moment, tossing out ideas in the name of the common good and exposing our collective consciousness. He is there as well, standing in line to contribute whatever idea he can. How on Earth did he get up there, by God? And now that he's there, there's no other way; there's no turning back. There's only one woman ahead of him, speaking. She proposes that we become a "political island," neither European nor African nor American, but a free-exchange zone of "trade and cultural innovation." When the woman is finished, it will be his turn. What is he going to say?

Imagine someone so timid that he can't even look you in the eyes, here in the seat of democracy. A fragile but well-meaning type like yourself—a normal human being. Deluded, disillusioned, depressed. Our country is a little like this, don't you think? Well then, what is it a country like ours could use—a factory of joy, a dream machine? No, let's not condemn ourselves to the fanciful aphorisms of fairy tales, please, no. What we need is a good utopia full of color. Do you like that? Will you vote for me? In the Assembly of the Republic, standing in the line of the citizen-revolutionaries, Americo ponders what he will say to the country.

His turn has come, they signal him to go up, and, in the blink of an eye he forgets everything. A huge blank. His heart leaps; there's an emptiness in the pit of his stomach. Okay, here he goes. His hands sweating, he ascends the fateful steps, stalling for time, and now here he is on the rostrum from where he can see "the beautiful rectangle by the sea," Portugal. Who would have thought? He adjusts the microphone, loosens his collar, and prepares to utter his first sentence.

Suddenly a cell phone starts ringing. An irritating sound—*ti-ti, ti-ti*—echoing throughout the amphitheatre, this great temple of democracy, sacred seat of the ongoing revolution. The ringing grows louder, the citizens in the gallery look at each other, disquieted. And then he realizes, how embarrassing, that the cell phone is his, he forgot to switch it off. The February 29th crowd looks at him with wicked eyes; there is an uneasy silence ....

Americo awakens, startled. He looks at his cell phone. Is it Carla Bruna's usual text? And suddenly he remembers: she's dead. On the television the common folk, wearing improbable clothing, speechify soundlessly. No, the message is from Joana. He can hardly believe it; it's Joana after all. He reads the phrase one time, then another.

13. Real Life

Three days later, Joana greets him at home as if nothing has happened. As if there had never been any problem, no scene on the staircase, no dirty laundry, no end of the world, as if Americo had simply left home and gone off to work—the conventional role of the husband who travels here and there to "earn a living"—and had now returned, just like that, the most natural thing in the world. In the blink of an eye everything is just as it was. All sweet smiles and small talk. "And the movie? How goes it? What do you think of the American director? Met any famous actors?"

"It's going well, thanks. And how are things here?"

"Everything's great," she says.

"The revolution … have you noticed anything different?"

"A little. On TV."

"On the way here, in the tollbooths, they were handing out sunflowers."

"Flowers will change the world."

"Nothing that hasn't happened before."

Joana turns on the television. "Do you want to watch the parliamentary marathon?"

Americo sits down on the sofa. "May I?"

"Make yourself at home," she says, with a beautifully wicked grin.

In his room Joachim dreams of gigantic Lego stars.

"This one," says Americo, referring to the woman about to take the Assembly podium. "I think I've seen her speak already."

"Isn't it forbidden to speak twice?"

"Perhaps 'forbidden' is a counterrevolutionary concept."

Joana turns towards him. "Is everything all right?"

"Yes, why?"

"Oh, nothing."

They watch the Assembly speeches in silence. All the channels are broadcasting the same images; only the lead-ins are different. On Channel 1, they're calling it *Revolutionary Emissions*. On Channel 2, *Special: February 29th*. On Channel 3: *The People Speak: A Marathon*. On Channel 4: *A New World*. Sitting side by side, Joana and Americo soon grow tired of anonymous people sputtering out solutions to the country's crisis.

"This will get us nowhere," she says, moving from the couch to her computer. Leaping numbers, garish graphics.

"What?" Americo asks, having heard his wife quite clearly.

But Joana doesn't turn around, hypnotized by the colorful rectangles on her computer screen. "Oh, nothing," she says. "Nothing." And then, after awhile: "Mariana and Mario are coming for dinner the day after tomorrow, is that okay?"

Americo switches off the televised close-up of "The People's Woman." "Oh, yes?"

He looks at her, arched reverently over the computer, as if she were praying to the God of the Internet, and is unable to suppress a cruel, burgeoning thought: What if Joana is taking him back solely to return to her normal social life?

Dinner with the Rodrigueses is proceeding wonderfully until he lets something slip. Joana picks it up right away. She tries to change the subject, to talk about what's right in front of them: the Argentine beef, the

French mushrooms, the shrimp from Matosinhos. But it's too late. Mariana Rodrigues asks him what exactly he means by the "old regime." Mario points his finger at him. "You! You're the most reactionary of all of us!" "Calm down," says Americo. "I didn't mean to offend anyone."

"We are no more 'old regime' than you are, if you must know."

"Of course not, Mario. Of course you aren't."

"So …," says Joana, " …do you know what they're charging these days for half a kilo of organic artichokes from Beira Baixa?"

Americo lifts his eyes toward their guests. "On the other hand, I must have hit a nerve. I've never seen our Mario so flustered."

"Fucking bastard!" says his friend, laughing, a laugh that takes all the effort he can muster.

The women exchange glances.

"Have you tried the wine?" asks Mariana.

Mario raises the glass to his nose but doesn't drink.

"And Zé Maria?" Joana interjects. "How is he doing? Is he sleeping okay? He was born quite big, am I right?"

"He's fine," says Mariana.

An imbecilic smile is still frozen on Mario's face. "Now that little guy's a true revolutionary …"

Upon hearing this, Mariana grimaces horrifically, as if she were repulsed by the smoked mushrooms on her plate. She does not approve of her husband saying such things about her newborn son. "Oh, you can't imagine what I went through giving birth to that sweet child." At first she addresses only her friend, but little by little she gathers Americo into her glance, gaining a larger audience for her story.

Mario goes back to sniffing the wine.

Americo takes note. "Uh-huh."

Mario looks over at him, but the actor has already shifted his attention to the Argentine beef.

Meanwhile Mariana continues talking nonstop. She recollects that she felt a small pain, at the base of her belly, then hailed a cab and went to the maternity hospital. She thought of calling Mario but, because she suspected that it was a false alarm, which might later prove a terrible letdown, she didn't. But, upon entering the maternity ward, she had a premonition, or maybe it was a slightly more severe but not yet intolerable pain, and sent him a text. She thought a text would be better: that way she could deliver the news without a big fuss, without the risk of emotional excess, and minimize any expectations.

"That message was a testament to her capacity for pithiness," says Mario. "A true haiku."

"A what?" asks Joana.

"You know," says Americo. "Those Japanese poems. Miniatures."

"Like bonsai?"

Fortunately Mariana doesn't hear her comment and goes on with her story. She says that, when she arrived at maternity, "sort of on the sly," she felt a little "adulterous." As if she had checked into some shady hotel without her husband knowing. A modern hotel, with white furniture and glass walls, atypical of Lisbon, in broad daylight.

And with that Joana's smile vanishes.

Americo looks over at his wife. Yup, the word "adulterous" did it.

But Mariana is unflappable; she rattles on. She even manages to stuff a mushroom in her mouth and continue talking without dispersing *salive français* all over the tablecloth that the hostess so fastidiously selected for the occasion. "When you get admitted over there ... well, they don't put you in bed right away. I mean, upstairs, in a room. First they make you fill out all that paperwork and, well, that's when it happened. In that idle time, hanging around, waiting around for the desk clerk to finish up all that bureaucratic stuff—you know, name, numbers, all that annoying crap blah blah blah—it was then that I sent that text to Mario. It was more out of boredom, really, than anything else."

Mario laughs a pathetic little laugh.

"But, suddenly, I felt something, something like a hot chill. Ickkk. Some kind of fluid was running down my legs, getting their nifty white floor all wet, how embarrassing. And there I was, standing in that puddle, panic-stricken, screaming my head off. I swear. I could only see the head of the clerk, all freaked out, peeking out from behind the counter, and on the wall, a drawing of a finger in front of a pair of lips, the symbol to keep quiet. And just then a nurse, super *simpatica*, showed up. She told me that it was nothing to worry about, that this was normal, and took me up in the elevator. And that was it. So somehow that text message to Mario was broken off. I must have pushed "Send" just as I started screaming, who knows? And afterwards I completely forgot about it. All the text said was, *To erase any doubt.* But so poetic, in its own way, wasn't it, darling? He figured everything out, just from that, and when Zé Maria came out ... I mean, *was born*, there was Papa Mario with the most petrified, most ... *melting* manner you can imagine, clutching my hand and saying, 'He has my eyes, he has my eyes ....' Incredible, isn't it?"

"Yeah," says Joana. "Incredible."

There is a brief silence; everyone is turned toward their plates. Dates from the Algarve, arugula from the Minho. Mario lifts his glass of wine to his nose, sniffs at it. Finally he takes a swig. When he sets down his glass, a question drops from his lips: "And the mystery of Carla Bruna?"

Americo stares at him from across the table. The next course has arrived: Revenge, served cold. The motherfucking son of a bitch. "They still don't know very much." The tone of his voice is lower than normal; he averts his eyes when he speaks. "The police haven't found anything yet." He must not look at Joana, under any circumstance. He can feel her face burning next to his. *Hold on, man, do not look at her.* That name has never been uttered between them, not even during their worst moments, not even during their most painful conversation the day Americo left the house. *Bear up, man, bear up.* Long seconds. Endless seconds.

———

He met her on the night of the day of the downpour. He was on his
way to catch a flight to Barcelona, to participate in a Mediterranean
drama festival, featuring a performance by the U theater troupe,
based on Fernando Pessoa's poem, "Ibis, Bird of Egypt." He was
playing an implausible and diverting character, the Indiana Jones of
Rua dos Douradores. He was quite curious to see how the Catalans
would receive such an offbeat project, but the Ibis never took off.
The bad weather conditions kept Portuguese planes grounded for
over thirty hours, and the retinue cleansed their souls with powerful
spirits at Club Erox.

"Buy me a vodka?"

It was the first time he laid eyes on her. "Who, me?"

"Thank you, I much appreciate it. Are you alone?"

"I'm with a group. They're off dancing. That bunch over there,
jumping up and down."

But the woman doesn't look at the dance floor. "You don't like
to dance?"

"I like to, but ...." Americo had never seen such strange eyes.
Black beams floating in bowls of milk. "I wanted to finish my drink."

"Would you like to dance with me?"

"Huh?"

"In private. I live nearby."

"Now? ... Oh, here they come, I have to go ..."

"Don't be nervous."

"I'm not, it's just that .... What's your name? I'm Americo."

"A pleasure, Americo," she says, squeezing his hand in a professional manner.

"Let's exchange phone numbers, so we can get together another
time, okay?"

"I don't have a cell. Give me your number. I'll ask a question and
then you'll come."

"A question?"

"Americo, come on, let's blow this joint, man!"

It's Franklin, an actor so tall and so stiff they once made him play the cherry tree in Chekhov's classic. Americo says yeah, he's coming, he'll be right there, and scribbles his phone number on a paper napkin. He slides it across the bar and sets it in front of her. The woman picks it up with two hands, as if it were a very fragile object that could, if improperly handled, disintegrate into thin air. She lingers for what seems an eternity. Americo can't take his eyes off her.

"Very well. Americo, right?"

"Right …," he says, pulling himself away. "But I really have to go …."

"My name is Carla Bruna."

If the fact of knowing this woman was one of his life's miracles, if fucking this woman would become a religion to him, then this was his first denial.

The company of actors, all so drunk they seem like low-budget imitations of that out-of-focus character played by Robin Williams in Woody Allen's *Deconstructing Harry*, applaud him on his way out of the club. "Bravo! Bravo! Encore! Encore!" Americo thanks them with a curtsy. "No, but seriously," says Oscar, a pudgy fellow with 3-D glasses who is the director of the U Theatrical Association. "Who's the dame?"

Americo smiles, as if it were no big thing, and plays along with the gag. "Oh … nobody."

The billboard off the freeway exit has been deteriorating for decades. Days and nights of rain and wind. Above the graying image of the laughing old folks, the words *Happy Rest* are now a morbid joke. Americo is not sure that going there was a good idea after all. What he is certain about is that his father won't recognize him, that he'll call him "Orestes" or "pygmy," and that he'll leave there more depressed than when he arrived. "Happy Rest." What sort of monstrous hand wrote those words?

There is nobody at the reception desk. Americo opens the door tentatively and comes upon an empty living room. Couches, tables, chairs, a television. How odd, everything deserted like this. Meanwhile two magazines lay open on a table, like fish who've leapt from the aquarium, leaving behind the impression of life. A coarse, irregular sound, off in the distance. Americo stops. The air conditioner? The wind on an upper floor? He goes down a wide corridor that smells of bleach, ascends the staircase. In the corner a lamp, illuminated. In front of him, another door. Americo takes a deep breath, twists a golden doorknob.

The coarse sound that has followed him since the first floor transforms itself into music. A Cuban number that sings of memories and *la sangre*. Americo can't believe his eyes.

A line of fifteen or twenty old folk, men and women, moving in a circle to the rhythm of the music. A kind of dance, the primitive kind. Clenched fists, waving arms, focused faces. And off to the side, just outside the circle, his father in a wheelchair. "Be these bodies!" he shouts. "You are only these bodies! That's it! That's it! Body, movement! Movement, body!" Christ, he's the fucking choreographer.

Americo doesn't move, doesn't speak. He waits for his father to spot him.

But he doesn't, of course. And wouldn't, even if he stood there like a statue for the rest of his life. His eyes are blind to anything outside the movement, outside the music.

No? Fluffing up his collar and jacket like someone picking himself up from a ridiculous fall, the son turns around, coughs quietly, and splits.

Back in Lisbon, stuck in traffic, he watches the rain against the dark clouds. What did he want out of that visit, after all? To see his father again? To verify his madness, to alleviate his own guilt? Does he believe that, given a moment alone with his father, a crack in the wall through which they could look at each other, man to man, without all the noise, his father could find the capacity to forgive him? Does he have the audacity to desire this, the succor of forgiveness? Does this mean that he's guilty? Guilty of what? If his father were to offer the words—"forgiveness," "I forgive," "I forgive you"—would he feel "cleaner, lighter," like in those ads for "women's things" on television? In any case, it was good to see him. His father, leader of the Happy Rest Revolution. Using whatever energy he's got left so that energy itself has its final thunderclap. The only salvation possible: to dance like crazy until you drop.

"How are you, behaving yourself?"

His mother looks at him as if she's never seen him before. She's watching a detective drama with her grandson on her lap.

"Oh, quite well. And you?"

"Me too, like always .... Isn't that a little too violent for him?"

On the TV screen, the detective sticks the barrel of his gun into the mouth of an old black man.

"Naah, it's fine. Joachim doesn't get it yet. You don't now, do you, dear?"

Joachim laughs at the sound of his grandmother's voice.

Americo picks up the kid. "I went to see Dad."

"Oh, did you?"

"It was nice seeing him."

"Really? Was he well?"

"He was content."

"And did he recognize you? Did he say anything special?"

"Well, not 'content,' exactly. He was enjoying himself. He said lots of things, yes. He was ... happy."

14. Aguas Livres

It's November and the city is covered with Christmas lights. In Carmo Square the trees resemble Michael Jackson's sequined gloves, giant hands reaching up for the sky. Americo is returning home from a walk to the Baixa with Joachim when he notices a woman headed in his direction. Her short, comical steps against the artificial light lend her figure the bearing of an insect. "Dr. Americo?" she says. She holds an absurd little piece of paper in her hand.

As he gets closer, Americo realizes that she is exceedingly thin, with protruding cheekbones and large, dark eyes.

"My name is Rosana."

"Do you want an autograph?"

"I'm her sister," she says, holding the paper out to him. "Well, I was."

Americo wants no part of any little piece of paper. He lowers his head, pushes Joachim's stroller forward.

"Please, read it," insists the woman. "I'd rather not speak in public."

"Have a good night. Good-bye."

"Not 'was.' I still am. We don't stop being sisters because she's dead, do we?"

Now he gets it. It's the eyes, of course. How is it possible? Americo didn't know she had a sister. The truth is he knew nothing about her life apart from what he saw and what he imagined. "You're ... Carla's sister?"

"Yes, I am," she responds, lifting up the paper as if to say, "That's what is written here."

Americo turns and takes a good look at her. She's a tragic version of the sizzling hot Bruna that he knew; his glorious love rendered in the form of an insect. Nonetheless, those eyes. A dark light that he thought had been forever extinguished.

"I see that I am surprise to you," Rosana says. She enunciates each syllable carefully, as if she had learned to speak from a correspondence course. "I don't wish to take up too much of your time. I would just like to ask your permission to contact you later. There's some information I would like to pass along. It's about Bru."

"Bru?"

"That's what our family called her. Princess Bru." Remembering this, Rosana offers up a rotten, craggy-toothed smile. "You're the only one I can trust, Dr. Americo, in order to get what—"

"Please, not 'Doctor', just call me—"

"In order to get this done, I can't trust anyone else. But it can't be today and it can't be here. Please, if you don't mind, can you write your number on the back of this paper?"

"Why don't we discuss it right here and now? There's no one around."

"Maybe I'm losing it but—I don't know ... these days I'm afraid of everything. I sense that there are people watching me in strange ways, from buses, on the sidewalk. ... I see shadows everywhere."

"It's just people walking by."

"When I show you, you'll understand." Then suddenly, pointing to the stroller: "What's his name?"

"Joachim. He's my son."

"Pretty name. But isn't he a little heavy for such a small thing?"

"Maybe. I never thought of that."

The woman's eyes, two black circles, are fixed on him. "Write your number down here, please."

Americo writes his number on the back of the paper. Rosana snatches the paper, folds it into quarters, thanks him with a slight nod of her head then backs away against the light. Short, stiff steps through the great lyrical trees.

A week later, Americo is in the living room taking care of Joachim, who stumbles all over the place, determined to break something. He is unsuccessful in getting him to sleep. After a half an hour of yelling, making his head feel like a balloon about to burst, he decides to throw in the towel—and Joachim picks up on this right away. Empowered by the sensation of triumph, the child wreaks havoc through the house wearing a somnambulant smile.

"Joachim, no! No, Joachim! Fuck, how many times do I have to tell you!"

The country has suffered through a revolution, envisioned for itself a whole new society while at the same time fearing a collapse into chaos, expulsion from the European Union, intervention by the IMF, occupation by UN peacekeepers, and, after several months of "the People's Parliament" and great uncertainty, finally scheduled "direct elections," in which any citizen over the age of sixteen can run. A thousand lofty dreams. And everything, in the end, has turned out more or less the same as before, with a "National Salvation" government formed by bureaucrats with solid resumes and without an ounce of shame.

Stuck at home, caring for their son while Joana flies off to "earn a living," Americo is like the country. More or less the same as before.

"Don't do it."

Leaning against the coffee table, Joachim grabs a vase. The numbered Japanese one that Joana paid an arm and a leg for. He looks at his father. May I? The wry little smile of someone who already knows the answer.

"No, no." Suddenly the cell phone rings. "Hello?"

"How are you, Doctor Americo?" says a woman's voice.

"Fine, thank you, but—"

"Today is a good day to have that conversation."

"What ... now?"

"No, not now."

"Oh, good. Because today I'm with my—"

"Meet you in an hour, at bus stop 229, right after the curve of the Aqueduct."

"The Aqueduct ...." Americo watches Joachim drag Mommy's delicate jar across the floor. "The Aguas Livres Aqueduct?"

It's chilling. On the phone, Rosana's voice sounds almost identical to Carla Bruna's. The only difference, perhaps, is the palpable breathiness beneath the words. The quickened breathing of an afflicted heart—like someone talking while looking over her shoulder at a dangerous corner. Like someone speaking, thinks Americo, on a burning telephone.

"A vitally important thing."

He leaves his son with the grandmother, with the excuse that "a vitally important matter has come up." It's no different from when Carla Bruna still breathed her regal breath and, in order to pay humble allegiance to her in Room No. 6, he had to invent meetings and rehearsals and bureaucratic appointments—he had to lie to Mother.

In the glass of the subway car, Americo watches his reflection. He sees a face suspended against the rushing walls.

But, all the same, this time it's true: something vitally important *has* come up.

"Good afternoon, ladies and gentlemen. Thank you very much for your attention."

A boy with an accordion and a small dog enters the car at the Avenida station. He smiles artfully, smelling of garbage. The people in the car look away.

The situation puts Americo on edge.

A joyful tune played with utter indifference. The dog dances woefully atop the red accordion, the instrument wheezing like a poor, emaciated old clown. The boy's smile is astounding. A bright, tidy smile, right out of a magazine ad. Americo would toss him some change if only it would shut him up for eternity.

Americo gets out at Santa Apolónia and heads for Bus Stop 229. Before leaving the house, he confirmed that the number corresponded to an actual bus, and that he could hop on that bus from there to the appointed meeting spot. On Google Maps, the Aqueduct appears as just an A inside a tiny balloon. But through the bus window, the city now streams past with an excessive, almost poignant, tangibility. Seated by the window, feeling as if he were suspended above the Earth, Americo sees the napes of necks, the tops of heads; hairlines, backs, legs. Scratches, fault lines, breaches, stains. It's one of those days when the winter sun seems to bring people and things into greater focus, making them appear truer to their actual selves.

It is only when the bus takes the steep, twisting descent toward the Aqueduct that Americo remembers the purpose of this outing and feels his stomach knot. The nervous, callow sensation of someone landing in a foreign country for the first time.

He is the only one that gets off at the stop. A nameless place, neither road nor street. A fallow African field from some French documentary. The orange lettering on the bus stop is like an extemporaneous element, a prop clashing with the tableaux of roadside vegetation and anonymous vehicles that enter and leave the city. The quietude of beasts more than of people. Americo steps off the bus. He keeps his head down and a close eye on where he walks.

The automatic door whooshes shut, the bus slowly vanishes.

The woman isn't there. He looks around. Nobody. A scene where anyone, including himself, would seem completely out of place. Fuck, what a perfect spot to get mugged.

"Doctor Americo?" says a voice behind him.

"Huh?"

"I didn't mean to startle you," says Rosana. "But here is not a good place to talk. Please, follow me."

Americo does what the woman says. "But don't call me 'Doctor,' okay?"

They proceed along a dirt path hidden amongst shrubs, very narrow and snaking upward. He looks at the ugly legs of his lover's sister, brown but somehow pale, skinny but too thick at the ankles. Every now and then, he detects the improbable odor of strawberry yogurt. Could it be her?

They pass by a tiny house with a satellite dish outside the window, and a few minutes later, they stop alongside a tragic old wall.

"This is it," says Rosana, facing her guest so as not to miss his reaction.

Americo smiles, not understanding.

Rosana squats down, produces a key from her shoe, and inserts it into a tiny wooden door set in the wall. The door is russet-colored, and looks like something right out of *Alice in Wonderland*. It's all so surreal that Americo feels like he's stepped into a dream.

He watches the woman open the door. The key must smell terribly. And what nonsense is this—putting a door in a wall?

Inside, a dense darkness. Rosana pulls a flashlight from her pocket and shines the light on a disorderly pile of clothes. It's a much more affecting sight than one would expect, a kind of artistic installation. For just an instant, Americo believes some creature will come scooting out from beneath the pile. It's as though the clothes are breathing.

Maybe it's only the light of the flashlight dancing on the rags.

And then, without warning, my God. Rosana sticks her hand inside the pile, slowly, with extreme caution, as if she were plunging her arm into a deep pool of mud. And as if she were afraid of something, as if that thing, that shabby pile of cloth, might rise up like some living thing, a diseased, dispassionate monster.

Rosana turns to face Americo—a look that seems to say nothing—and lifts her hand.

She's holding a black, hardcover notebook. Americo looks at the exhumed object and can't help but feel a certain sense of disappointment. He was expecting a frightful and definitive Truth. On the cover of the old notebook, it reads *Bru*.

"This is it," says the woman, acting surprised.

"Can I look at it outside?" Americo asks. "It's so dark in here …."

She hands him the notebook and trains the flashlight directly on him. "You better not," she says, as if she trusts and mistrusts him all at once.

Americo turns his face, his eyes hurting from the light. He looks at the black rectangle he holds in his hands. Is this all there is?

"Don't be afraid," she says.

With the peevish air of the faithlessly penitent, Americo opens the book.

Dear Diary …

On the first page, these two impossible words. And, following them, names, names, and more names. Pages filled with telephone numbers, dates, initials, *names*.

Americo recognizes some of them. Big, resounding names. Politicians, bankers, athletes, television personalities.

"Don't fret, Doctor, you're not in there."

"No?"

"To Carla, the Doctor was …"

"Please, call me Americo."

"Was … another story. 'If there's ever a problem, go talk to him,' she used to tell me. 'He will help you, for sure,' she said. And then I would ask her, 'Problem how? What problem?' She would say, 'Oh.' And just shrug her shoulders."

"Are these all the ones she …"

"She and others she knew, of course. There are more than two hundred names in there! The Doctor doesn't think my sister could …"

"Of course not."

"And all of them in there have been validated. Those she wasn't sure about, she didn't put in the notebook. This story was for her protection."

Americo closes the notebook, hands it back it to Rosana. He thinks of the woman's words: *This story was for her protection; the Doctor was another story .... This story, another story ....*

But Rosana refuses it. "In the end, it didn't protect her at all," she says, half-smiling.

Sensing her pressing in on him, Americo tries to step back, but there isn't enough room. Her hair exudes a powerful odor. Detergent? Vinegar? With a terrible dread he feels the hand of his dead lover's sister on his chest.

"Please, Doctor."

"What do you ..."

"Find out who killed Bru. It's in there, I'm certain of it. He's in there somewhere, somewhere amongst those names," she says, pointing to the notebook that the actor holds in his hand. "Now, you'd better go."

Suddenly, the night. Once outside, Rosana and Americo stop to admire the landscape. They stand there without speaking for several seconds. Far from the buildings and the streets, the dark sky descends to the earth, like a black curtain in a rehearsal hall.

"It's all a great madness, isn't it?" says the woman.

"What?"

"You know ... the country. First revolution, now confusion."

Americo nods. "Good-bye."

"See you."

They shake hands and Rosana points him toward a path less circuitous than the one they came in by: go around the little house and then descend in a straight line to the road. She tells him that it "might be best" if he keeps the notebook hidden inside his clothing.

Americo tucks it close against his chest and goes around the cottage. Then he turns back, in a gesture of farewell. He wants to recall everything exactly as it is, as if the memory of the most minute details will somehow protect him.

Seen from behind, the little house has a rounded shape, an igloo made of brick and timber, leaning hard against a large wall. Standing by the door, the woman raises the flashlight above her head and points its white light toward the great descent. She asks Americo if he's okay, if he can see the path down to the road. He says yes and waves good-bye, although, in the darkness of the Lisbon outback, Rosana looks less like a human and more like a giant insect with one beaming eye.

A cold wind kicks up. The shrubs appear to genuflect.

"Good-bye, thanks!" Americo yells back, but the woman has already vanished.

Keeping his eyes fixed on the ground in front of his feet, as a way to keep his fear in check, the actor walks down the hill. When he gets to the road, he heads for the bus stop. He waits. After a while, he begins hearing strange sounds that make him think of beasts devouring other beasts—he must get away from there. He takes off on foot. From there back up to the city it should take him about ten minutes? Fifteen? More?

And so he goes, long strides, his torso leaning forward, climbing up the shoulder.

Should anyone with a suspicious manner approach him, what will he do? Take off running down the middle of the road? Would he rather be stabbed by a nervous assailant or crushed against the mud flaps of a Swedish semi? And what, exactly, should he consider a "suspicious manner"? Not many cars pass by at this hour, so he stands a pretty fair chance of getting away without being run over. Here comes one now, its headlights enlarging like a pair of blind eyes.

Americo picks up his pace, speeds up the road. *Nothing's going to happen, nothing's going to happen.*

When he gets to Spanish Plaza, he breathes a sigh of relief. At last. He turns right toward the Marques but stops at the beginning of the slope where once, years ago, there was a gas station. He is exhausted, sweating.

Facing the wind, his hand clutching his chest as if he were in some kind of pain, Americo waits for a taxi to appear amidst the parade of cars passing by. What a fucking hell of a story. A lousy little cabin in the middle of nowhere, a secret notebook full of important names, the smell of it all. The tragic version of Carla Bruna illuminating a dirt path in the miserable outskirts of Lisbon. A taxi appears in the distance; he raises his arm.

"Don't take that cab," says a man's voice.

Rosado is on the sidewalk, his arms held tight against his body, as if he had just been teleported from the Federal Police station. "Do not take it."

Instinctively, Americo crosses his arms, protecting the notebook hidden against his chest. "Look who's here," he says, feeling the cold, hard cover against his skin.

The inspector doesn't smile. His expression is intensely focused, as if, in the triangle formed by the eyes and mouth of the actor, there was a question flickering. Over by the curb, Nogueira signals the cab to keep going, a gesture made with a strange, disdainful disgust, as though his hand were flipping through invisible pages. And the cab driver, the prick, obeys.

"I'm afraid you'll have to accompany us to headquarters," says Rosado, his voice rising.

"Me?"

"But first we are going to read you your rights and all that legal mumbo-jumbo that the new 'revolutionary'"—he carefully enunciates the word, separating each syllable, as if introducing a new, obscure term to a nursery school class—"regime obliges us. It's the law."

"It's the law," repeats Nogueira, shaking his head for emphasis.

"But why," asks Americo, "am I being … arrested?"

"Your name, sir, is Americo Santos Sousa Silva Abril, is it not?"

"But what have I done, goddammit?"

15. Face of the Monster

He was in his early teens, standing on a chair in a big room with streamers hanging from the ceiling. Was he fourteen? Or fifteen?

From behind the closed window, Americo looks at the yellowish, white streets. The city is absurdly quiet; buildings, trees and poles moving backwards. "That cloud is following us." Who just said this? Suddenly, another street, a different light, and the face appearing in the glass is the face of someone else. It frightens him; just a reflex. How strange, the eyes superimposed on the seeing. Father, it was Father who used to say, when they were driving somewhere and the silence was too long, "That cloud is following us."

"But isn't the sky all blue?"

It was a Carnival party and Americo was masquerading as the Face of the Monster. His parents had brought the hideous thing from London. "It was quite a hit over there," his father said. "It was on sale," his Mother told him. A green mask with wrinkles and warts and rounded holes for the eyes, nose, and mouth. For the party, billed pompously as "A Carnivalesque Mask and Costume Ball," Americo dressed in his grandfather Abilio's coat, a pair of his father's old weekend gardening boots, and the green mask of the London monster. A vague and repugnant face; a mixture of toad, Martian, and old crone. Nobody would recognize him wearing that mask.

He asked to be dropped off before the bend in the road. He preferred to walk to the school gate. If his friends saw him get out of that car, a white Fiat 127 with a dent on the right side, they would recognize him right away. "I'll go the rest of the way by myself, no problem."

His mother turned toward the back seat. "Are you sure?"

The walk alone to the school was like a chamber of horrors. He suffered twenty or thirty meters of sidewalk with that green head weighing on his shoulders, aging him countless years. Was he sixteen? Or fifteen?

At the entrance, the gatekeeper asks for his ticket. Americo hands him the tiny translucent slip without speaking. A group of classmates approach him. "Who are you? Hey, who's this dude?" Clowns, punks, pirates. Shielded behind the Face of the Monster, Americo smiles, but says nothing. He wants to see what will come of all this. No one realizes it's him; how cool.

The situation exhilarates him for the first ten minutes. Then it begins to get on his nerves. Americo the Teenage Monster is not quite able to formulate the thought, but he senses that something's not quite right in all this, that his friends aren't trying hard enough. Inside the hot, suffocating London mask, he gets the feeling that maybe he doesn't really matter much to them. A gossamer gargoyle.

"Are you sure?"

Americo stands frozen, alone at the ball, studying the crowd.

It was the time of all doubt, of questioning everything. The time to question every phrase, every word, everything with the odor of a law or the whiff of a lesson. To rehearse one's movements, to conceive of a recognizable and original style. To figure out what to do with one's hands when walking down the street, what to do about the wild notions bristling from within. To check your face in the mirror a thousand times a day. A face of imprecise contours, all too white and splattered with zits. As if he could vanish from within, lose himself entirely, as if he ran the risk of dying if he didn't look in the mirror for a certain length of time, a few minutes, an hour. At fifteen, Americo is an acne-ridden face dreaming of such vague and generic things as "roaming freely in the world" and such concrete and particular things as "Patricia's naked body."

"Hello, Americo."

But the right moment never comes. That is, when the "right moment" comes, a certain sliver of his heart always fails him. "Hello, Patricia ...." The boldness of a gesture, a question to throw her off balance. A *presence of mind*, to use the proper expression. Being in the world is so complicated. There are no mirrors, no defenses. It's like driving down an endless road made of only eyes and sunlight. Easier to shut yourself up in your room, to retreat into music, writing poetry, sketching; to suffer in dreams.

"You think we're not going to figure out who you are?" says the Witch.

He turns and looks. It's her. "What?" The Witch is the Patricia of his sweetest nightmares.

"Ah, so you speak. I got a word out of you."

"Uh ..."

"And yet another."

The Face of the Monster shakes its head.

Patricia the Witch is amused. She laughs.

He feels so calm behind the mask. Behind the window glass, Americo looks at the reflections, remembers. It was February, but in his memory it seems like summer. The school gymnasium, which, at night, was a much better, much more dangerous place, the music turned up loud. He stands on the chair and opens his arms as if to say: *Ta-daa!* And there at his feet, the wonderful Witch. Streamers of red, blue, and yellow form endless W's and the music grows louder and louder. What's this? A waltz? Perhaps a facetious notion from some smart aleck teacher. Lording himself over the small masked multitude, Americo stretches out his arms, their self-appointed champion. A Champion of Terror, a

Carnival Christ, the Monster's Face of fanciful, impossible, teenage love.

"Miss Patricia ... may I have the honor of this dance?"

Later, of course, he would go through his Al Pacino phase, his Jean-Paul Belmondo phase, his Luis Miguel Cintra phase; later, of course, he'd have his doubts, his demurrals, his despair, his dropouts, his resurrections; but it was there, in that instant, disguised as a Horrible Beast, that he discovered he wanted to be an actor, that he was an actor.

"No need to be such a gloomy Gus," says Nogueira, sitting next to him in the back seat of the Opel.

"What?" says Americo. Outside, mixed in with his reflections from the interior of the car, the white building revolves slowly, just like an idea that, at long last, reveals itself to him, and swirls within.

"We don't want to, by any means, put you out," adds Rosado, seated up front in the passenger seat. The driver, a young man with Slavic features, allows the trace of a smile. Rosado shoots him a stern look, and the young man's smile vanishes. "We are not here to upend anyone's life," proclaims the inspector from the bow. "Our only objective is to serve the Truth and the Revolution."

16. Dialogue

"That's my name," says Americo. He sits in a wooden chair—back straight, hands resting on his thighs—in a small, gray, square room.

"We apologize," says Nogueira. "'But you must say all this to the camera before we begin the actual interrogation.'"

The two inspectors stand and observe him with an academic patience. As if Americo were a rare bird and even the slightest flutter might prove revelatory. A blinking of the eyes, a dry swallow. A turn of face, a knitting of brow. Nogueira clears his throat and turns to his colleague to see if he's picked up any clues.

Rosado keeps his eyes trained on the suspect.

"I am innocent," sighs Americo. "I'm tired of telling you—"

"You're certainly not too impressed by any of this," says Rosado. His face is flushed, his nose and cheeks ruddy, as if a few minutes of self-imposed silence had caused an accumulation of blood around his mouth. "An actor must prepare himself to act before the camera, isn't that so?"

Americo holds firm, keeps his face perfectly still, focuses on the simple mechanics of inhaling and exhaling.

Nogueira attempts to cough and fails, resulting in a kind of discordant "*acch*."

"This is very serious," says Americo.

"You're absolutely right," says Rosado, adjusting his pompadour. "When a suspect attempts to withhold possible evidence of a crime, that is a very serious matter indeed."

Americo looks at Nogueira—is he really saying this?

But Nogueira turns his head.

"What are you talking about?" he yells at Rosado. "Are you referring to the notebook?" And, turning to face the camera suspended in the ceiling: "Are you talking about the notebook filled with prominent names that you stole from me when you kidnapped me in the street? Is that what you're referring to, Inspector?"

"Please, calm yourself."

"Let it be. Nogueira. Turn the thing off and shut the door."

Nogueira looks at his colleague, hesitates for a moment. His eyes have an eerie glow.

He takes two steps toward the wall, reaches up and switches off the camera. Then he turns toward Rosado and nods his head, as if to say: "Done."

"Very well," says his colleague, with a bogus grin.

Nogueira locks the door, turning the key once, twice.

"May I?" asks Rosado.

Nogueira looks at Americo, who has just risen from his chair. "Let's go, buddy ...."

Americo returns the gaze, but as if he doesn't see or hear him.

"Americo?" says Nogueira, in the somewhat desperate tone of the surgeon who realizes he's losing his patient for no apparent reason.

Meanwhile, Rosado closes in on the actor.

Coming out of his daze, Americo turns to face him. He's so close he can smell him: an explosive mixture of too much perfume and too few baths. "Sons of bitches."

"Relax," says Nogueira.

"It's time," says Rosado.

Americo grabs the chair to defend himself. He is dripping wet, as if a bucket of sweat had been dumped on his head.

"We're going to tell you the truth. It just so happens that, be-cause of the 'revolution,' because of the new 'revolutionary regime,' everything over here has gotten a little complicated ...."

"Keep your voice down, man," says Nogueira.

"And we received a direct order, from above, to detain you and confiscate the notebook."

"An order ... from whom?" Americo asks.

"We don't know," answers Nogueira.

"I can't say for sure," says Rosado. "Someone very high up. A major player."

Americo puts down the chair and sits.

"The problem is that with all this upheaval, the 'revolution' and such ... this whole changeover has rocked the boat in such a way that our situation here has become quite unstable, if you get my drift. This station where we work is at risk every day, all day. All fucking day. We've seen it happen to our own. One errant word, one joke taken the wrong way, and off you go.

"For instance," Nogueira adds, "if you say the word 'revolution' with even the slightest touch of irony."

"That's right," says Rosado.

"Just an example."

"Got it, thank you very much."

"But ...," Americo looks at the sad, Portuguese faces of the po-licemen. He tries to calm himself, looks for the right words. "You mean you're arresting me without ... cause, just because some big-wig wants the notebook with the names to disappear?"

"What names?" Rosado asks, playing innocent.

"And don't talk so loud," says Nogueira.

"The culprit is right there amongst those names!" Americo brings his hands to his head. "How can this be happening?"

Rosado observes him with his nose raised upward—as if he was guessing at the actor's posture in a game of charades.

"So this is what we achieved with February twenty-ninth? This is what we end up with?"

"Yup," says the inspector with the pompadour. "But let's not dwell on that. As for the subject at hand ... we did only what we were ordered to do. We brought you here and we confiscated the notebook, but do not worry."

"What have you done with it?"

"With whom?"

"Not with *whom*! With what! With the notebook!"

Rosado zips up his jacket. "We passed it along, through the proper channels, to our immediate superior who, have, no doubt, in turn, passed, or will soon pass, it up to the *eminence grise* who made the initial phone call."

"Who?" says Nogueira.

"The one who gave the order to give the order. I still don't have a name."

Americo gazes at him wearily. He too is speechless. He looks like he is suffering from a terrible hangover, all tousled and pale.

"But, never fear, let me finish—this big fella right here and myself—we will pursue this lead, follow this trail in the investigation. The trail of the notebook names, that is. Unofficially, of course."

"Of course," repeats Nogueira.

"And we won't lose sight of the trail of that kingmaker's phone call. To see where it all leads ... *capiche*?

Americo keeps quiet, biting his lip.

"Very well then," concludes Rosado. "You may take him now, Nogueira."

"I can go?" asks the actor, with a childlike delight.

Nogueira leads him away. They pass through two hallways with several doors, then down a long silent corridor. Everything—the walls, the floor—is colorless. Americo doesn't know where to look. White lamps strung along the ceiling, an homage to abandoned ideas. Nogueira doesn't look at him. He answers yes to every question. A dry, monotonal, robotic "yes."

"Have they been doing any construction?"

"Is this still part of the Federal Police?"

"Is this the way out?"

The policeman's shoes go *clop, clop, clop.*

At the end of the corridor, another door, and another small, gray foyer. Nogueira stops. Americo looks at him. Facing the empty hallway, the policeman states the day, the hour, then recites various random numbers. Americo looks up in search of a camera or a listening device of some sort, but sees nothing. "Is this the usual … procedure?"

The policeman doesn't respond. He opens one of the six identical doors and, with a slight tilt of his head, indicates the exit.

Americo enters into a dark room, and Nogueira shuts the door.

"Hey! What is—"

The sound of a big, fat key spinning in the keyhole. Once, twice.

17. Monologue

There's no point in screaming. This is no mistake. In the darkness, Americo stops pounding. There's no point hurting his fists against the cold door.

He backs against the wall and sits.

Maybe the inspectors will come back soon with an explanation. They had to put on a show for their superiors, to convince them that they were really, truly teaching him a lesson. That they were pushing him to the brink to extract some information from him—a false confession, a loose word, whatever—just some fragment of speech that the bosses could spin, twist, and retwist until it fits into their narrative. Every revolution has its scapegoats, and he's drawn the short straw. No, it can't be. Naah, the inspectors won't let him stay in here too long, in the cold, in the dark, clueless, incommunicado. A dank chill rattles his bones.

Americo stands up. He cups his hands over his nose and mouth, trying to warm himself with his breath. What if they forget about him? What if, amidst all their work, all those added layers of bureaucracy, all that extra red tape spawned by the new regime—who knows how many reports and stamps and initials and signatures?—the inspectors completely forget about him and leave him there to suffer? It's like being sealed away in an underground tomb. "Hey! Please!" The walls are blind, the door made of thick steel. Even if there were someone on the other side, they couldn't hear him. Americo sits down.

He plays games of tic-tac-toe in his head. He sings every song he can remember. He does calisthenics. He twirls his arms. He swivels his head, first to the right, then to the left. He stretches his legs. He paces back and forth, trying to keep warm.

His eyes have already adjusted themselves to the dark: a cube, they've locked him in a cube. A miniscule fucking cube. Four steps ahead, four on either side, and the ceiling just above his head. No room to think, no space to breathe.

Americo shuts his eyes tightly. The sadness that seizes him is one of profound desolation—an absolute, unyielding tedium. How much more of this can he take?

He does push-ups, something he remembers from an old movie. A prison flick in which someone says that physical exercise is essential to survival, that to maintain one's sanity, retain some measure of self-esteem, one must have objectives and a daily routine. He says it aloud so as not to forget: "Objectives. Routine." He does twenty push-ups, rests, does twenty more. What was the name of that movie? Who played the lead?

He unrolls a camping mat that is lying against the Primary Wall. This is what he dubs the wall across from the door, the others being Right Wall, Left Wall and Door Wall. He pictures Rosado inspecting his freshly swept cell. Giving the rolled-up mat a weak kick and making a lame remark about his pathetic camping gear. On second thought, no, the inspector won't even show up. "You can take him now," he'll say to some faceless subordinate, with the tone of someone who detests such inconvenient little details. Attending to the prisoner, turning the key, reading him his rights. "Re-vo-lu-tion," he'll say, slicing off each syllable so as not to choke on the word. The son of a bitch.

He lies on his side. He folds his arms across his chest. Whose hands are now clutching the notebook of Carla Bruna? The black book in which that vivacious woman so assiduously recorded names, dates, places. The notebook, dear God, that proves my innocence.

But he doesn't sleep. He can't help but think of his dead lover's sister on top of that hill. The insect-woman watching him through the dense darkness, her eye a beacon of light.

And what must Joana be doing at this very moment? She has certainly noticed him missing by now. Does she have any idea where he is, locked away for no reason? Has she spoken yet with Murilo, asked his help in all matters concerning the court, the police, the press? Or, my God—does she think he's run off with another woman, betrayed her yet again?

He pictures her on the couch, with a glass of wine by her side, watching an American TV show about doctors or cops or murderers just to keep from crying. He sees Joachim beneath his baby comforter, sleeping, getting further and further away from him, little by little, day by day (so much time lost), dreaming dreams in which his father never appears. He sees (and this makes no sense) an enormous, glowing, slimy, worm slithering between the furniture strewn about the house—who left it in such a state?

"Someone! Help! I'm in here!" He screams, pounding against the door with his fists and his feet. "Help! Help me! Somebody, please, I need help!"

But no one hears a thing.

Alone, in the dark. He squats at the toilet against Left Wall and lets loose all the shit that's been backing up inside him. He sobs, but not out of sadness.

You know it's night, even in the dark. In the dark you know it's night when men open the door and drag you by the arms, by the legs, by the hair, to an identical room, this one blazing with light, and tie you to a chair and fasten multi-colored wires to your chest, your head, the soles of your feet, and the wires are connected to a comical little contraption that scares the fuck out of you. In the dark you know it's night if the room is too bright and the light is too bright and its beam is focused directly on you, penetrating into you so intensely it hurts your eyes and your brain and, after all that time shut away without seeing a thing, or seeing only the flimsiest, most tenuous shadows, it is almost as if you imagined them. In the darkness, beyond the light, you know a man stares at you without speaking until you yearn for a question from him, any question, so that you can tell him everything, answer everything, even those questions that you don't know the answer to, even if you have to invent people to rat out, because you are already way past the point of resistance. In the dark another man will press a button on the machine and you will feel something surge inside you and you will know it is not good. In the dark you want to say you are guilty, just so they'll stop, of course, but also because it's true, because, after all the terror-sweat has begun dripping down your naked body, the truth is thus, the truth has become something else and now, yes, you are guilty. In the dark you say this, you want to say this, but no one asks you any questions, and in these officious environs it is proper etiquette that, when you speak the truth without a legally sanctioned question directed at you, this "truth" cannot be authenticated, is never, in fact, considered, except, of course, for the purpose of proving malicious intent, flouting of procedure, or insubordination, for providing responses to questions that have not been sanctioned, and therefore, not asked, guilty or otherwise. In the dark you are guilty, of course. In the dark there is someone who watches you without speaking and someone else who, very gingerly, tears off the sticky tape and repositions the multi-colored wires, moving the one from your chest to your testicles, the ones from the soles of your feet to your neck and the one from your forehead to your anus. In the dark one's sense of humor becomes excruciatingly wicked. In the dark. It's in the dark that you are going to die.

But before you lift up your head and open your mouth, a thick liquid oozes out of you that is either saliva or blood or neither, you can't tell, you clench your lips until—feeling an intense pain in the muscles of your face, as if, at that moment, you became the master of every single little nerve ending in your body and every trivial movement in your mortal being tore, multiplied by a thousand, through the limit of your consciousness—you spit. And, in the dark, you miss the target.

Americo wakes up screaming.

Then, suddenly, he stops. He's still there, in solitary. He's been sleeping, but this is no dream. Everything is the same, everything is dark. Is it morning? How long did he sleep? And what if the nightmare becomes reality? If, just outside, on the other side of the door, the police are waiting for him to grow fatigued so they can bust in, drag him by the hair through the corridors, and torture him in the room of intense light until he says that he's the culprit, he's guilty, guilty of everything, it was him, all him.

He's extremely cold. He should have gone on sleeping; awake he feels a terrible chill. He rubs his hands against his chest in an attempt to keep warm. He rubs himself everywhere. Legs, arms, ears.

He lies down again. He shuts his eyes, concentrates, tries to think of a landscape. Somewhere outdoors, a deserted place where nothing happens. A peaceful place. He should go back to sleep to escape the cold, so that nothing will happen to him. His throat hurts.

He opens his eyes. Total darkness.

Darkness everywhere, always; though somehow a tiny but very intense light, a microscopic sun, appears on the ceiling. Americo looks from one side of the room to the other and the light follows his gaze. He must be going mad. He stands up. He looks at the wall directly in front of him. There is no light.

Yet there it is. Yes, it's there. If he looks up, or down, or left, or right. It's a light, an honest-to-goodness light. Absurdly, Americo raises his hand to his forehead to see if someone fastened a lamp between his eyes, some sort of trickery that might explain everything. His skin feels dry and coarse. Beyond this, he feels nothing in particular.

It's like the reflection from his watch off the light of the window. He remembers being at home with Joachim and pointing out the circle of light on the wall. "Look at that little light. Up there. What is it? It's a ball. Look, the ball's moving. Look at the little jumping ball of light. Beautiful, isn't it? What is it?"

Nothing. Nobody.

"Hello."

"Hello," Americo answers back. Then it dawns on him: that was Paul Giamatti's voice. He's sitting right next to him on the white camping mat.

"My name is—"

"I know who you are, of course. I know all too well."

"How well?"

"Very well. Perfectly well."

"Ah, yes," says the American actor as though another thought had popped into his head.

"I like it. Your work, that is. Very much."

"Oh, well, thank you very much."

"No, I'm not saying it just to say it. It's the truth."

"Wow."

Americo is flustered, at a loss for words. He smiles. Paul Giamatti is both better-looking and uglier in person. "You've brought a light with you."

146 | Jacinto Lucas Pires

"A 'light' did you say?"

"It's that thing they always say about the truly charismatic. That they bring, or seem to bring, a certain light with them. How is it you speak Portuguese?"

"You're only hearing me in Portuguese."

Americo looks around, as if, on the walls, on the ceiling of his confinement, he might find an explanation for all this. "I see …"

"Interesting space you have here. Limited, but interesting. Of course, limitations are always interesting. Don't you agree?"

"Yes, I think so." Without taking his eyes off the American, Americo spends a few seconds considering the notion of limitations and how they relate, specifically, to his own life. He appears to be hypnotized. "It depends."

"Do you know I'm also an actor?"

"I should say so!"

"Not at all. We are one and the same."

"But it's curious, quite curious, that you touched on this topic."

"Sorry, but I haven't touched a thing."

"No, it's just an expression. It just means that—"

"The first time I acted in a play, in college, my character had to pray. It was very difficult. I was inexperienced, of course, and praying in public, on stage, seemed an absolutely formidable, if not impossible, undertaking. In rehearsals I tried affecting a pious demeanor, hands clasped, raising and lowering my eyebrows, my chin trembling, but nothing worked. A big nothing inside."

"I see."

"Until, after the third or fourth rehearsal, I explained my problem to the director."

"Here we call him *encenador*"

"And do you know what he said?"

"The director?"

"Kneel."

"That's it?"

"It was a miracle."

"A 'miracle'?"

"I figured out how to pray on stage and discovered, right there, what I wanted to do with my life."

"What?" says Americo, turning to the other side. Did he just hear a noise? "Is someone there?" he asks, in the direction of the door. Nothing. Silence.

Only his breathing, and the breathing of Giamatti.

And, when he turns back to the American, he's not there. He's vanished. How is it possible? Americo looks around. Yes, the confinement is solitary again. He's gone. Did he, could he have passed through the wall like some phantom, some special effects illusion?

Before he can fully picture this scenario—Paul Giamatti traversing the thick stone wall with the self-possession of a great actor—two big goons grab him and carry him out of the cell.

"But where ... who the ...?"

They are young, white, their faces unblemished, without character. They carry him through a corridor with utter seriousness, looking straight ahead. Is it fear he feels, or hatred? Their shoes go *clop, clop, clop*. Is this the live performance of what he rehearsed in his dream, in his nightmare? Americo turns from one to the other, seeking answers. An explanation, a look. But it's useless; he's a thing to them. A thing that walks and screams.

"Where are you taking me!"

18. Lordstar

Sitting on the sofa, with his arm around his wife, Americo watches the interview he gave to Channel 1. It's amazing how a public network managed to bring together all the worst aspects of the private stations. A studio set full of colors, flashing lights, and tricky contrivances, a true monument to bad taste and visual bombast; and scrolling beneath, with an equal degree of import, news and advertisements, culture and business, revolutions in the Arab world and lunchtime soap operas, not to mention a hysterical anchorwoman with ridiculous cleavage.

"And now, ladies and gentlemen, my good friend, Americo Abril!"

On the screen Americo looks out at the audience. In the studio bleachers, men and women, the young and the middle-aged, the middle class and the lower-middle class, all dressed in their Sunday finest, as if for an after-church picnic, but without the church. Is this what the revolution has come to, people sitting quietly, applauding when they're told to applaud, laughing when they are shown the sign that says *laugh*?

On the sofa Americo comments on how bad the program is. Joana agrees.

"So, at the outset, before I go any further, I want to ask you, how does it feel, now that you are free, and, on top of all that, now that you are the Lordstar?"

"Well, this was a name given to me by the newspapers after I got out of prison, but it seems to me what is really important—"

"Yes! Tell us a bit more about that. When you got out of those brand new high-security facilities built to house counterrevolutionary terrorists, you told the reporters outside that you believed you had 'seen God' and that, during that brief period of time you were deprived of your freedom, your view of the world and of humanity shifted radically."

"No, what I said was that I had seen a—"

"Now let's take a look at some of that footage! That moment, or rather, that *historic* moment when Americo Abril is released, having been cleared of the terrible charges hanging over him in the Death of The Bod affair."

Americo on the sofa watches Americo on TV watching the historic Americo exiting the prison. Joana kisses him and, in these past tense images, Murilo gives him little pats on the back. The three of them—the accused, the lawyer, and the wife—head toward the waiting car while a small battalion of cameramen, photographers, and journalists block their path.

"Do you consider yourself a political prisoner?"

"Will you be suing the new regime?"

"Are the accommodations nice inside?"

Americo hesitates, not knowing which question to answer. Joana takes his hand; they exchange affectionate smiles. Behind them, Murilo squeezes the papers under his arm like an obsequious man Friday. Americo faces front and addresses the crowd: "Inside these walls, I was visited by ... by a ... vision, a voice, that told me that, whenever we face adversity, we must kneel."

The studio audience gives Americo a round of applause. Sheepishly, Americo returns the applause. The show host looks like she's just won the lottery. "What a fantastic story! The actor who we first portrayed in the press as an adulterer, a murderer, and an assailant of journalists, has transformed into an angel who speaks with God!"

Americo tries to correct her. "No, I didn't exactly speak with—"
"A miracle! God told him to kneel, and he believed, he got down on his knees, and … he was freed!"
"No, I didn't quite get on—"
"He got down on his knees and found salvation! A big round of applause, folks, for Americo … Abril!"

The public will not stop applauding. The people—happy, moved—stand on their seats: young and old, men and women. Americo thanks them. He places his hands on his chest, as if to say, "I hold you all in my heart," and smiles, red-faced.

He's ashamed, yes, but he doesn't know what for. Because of that tacky gesture with his hands on his chest, or for something worse?

Watching all this from the couch, Americo sighs. At the time, during his "historic" moment of liberty, there was truth in what he said; those words were the truest, the best, the most honest he could come up with. But now, seeing everything in retrospect, on television, the whole thing seems fraudulent and, even worse, boring boring boring. "How sad, don't you think?"

But Joana has fallen asleep. Her eyelids are smooth as milk.

He grabs the remote, turns off the television. He embraces his wife. A familiar, pleasant, scent. Lemon? Chamomile? It's all to the good. Now he is the Lordstar and has offers from three producers for two prime-time soap operas and one cell phone commercial. Lead roles, major cache. Everything now is fine and dandy.

On the switched-off televison, a little red light.

Americo leans back. He runs his hand across his scalp, combs back the few hairs on the side of his head. He is so very tired, but he can't manage to close his eyes. That cursed light.

He can't stop thinking of what Rosado told him that day. Just before they sent him back into the streets, even before he was officially declared innocent, while his release papers were being notarized and he was pacing back and forth, passing the time in that pre-fab office that smelled like an old waiting room in a dentist's office

"Please accept my apologies," says the inspector, reaching out to shake his hand.

Americo looks at him in silence.

"I am convinced that you are innocent," Rosado declares, retracting his hand. "But just by an increment. Forgive the rhyme. At any rate, don't let it worry you. We are classifying the case as 'political' and closing it for good. Be well."

On the sofa Americo stares at the red light. What the fuck did he mean by "just by an increment?"

On Saturday Joana takes him for a walk to Chiado. They eat Italian ices and buy DVDs of television shows. Joachim points at him from the stroller and says something that sounds like "Da" or "Dee." Joana claps delightedly. "Did you hear that? He said 'Daddy!'"

"Is that what he meant?"

"Don't be silly. That was his first time, it's official! Now come on, 'Daddy,' take a picture!"

The actor smiles and points his cell phone at the kid. "Come on, Joachim, say it again. Say it one more time and this time, smile when you say it, okay? So you look handsome on Daddy's phone. Say it now, 'Da-dee,' 'Da-dee ....' Oh, so now you won't say it?"

That night, in bed, Joana pulls him toward her, wraps herself around him, strokes him, whispers dirty things in his ear. "Come over here, my triple X ...."

Americo feels like a bucket of cold water has been poured into his soul. *XXX*? He's never mentioned this to anyone. It wasn't printed in any newspaper or magazine. The police didn't know. He didn't even tell Murilo. What did she mean? It's not possible. Joana? My little Joana? Could she have found the text on his cell and—no, no it's not possible. There's no way. No, no, no. No and no.

Joana kisses his neck, nibbles on his earlobes, tugs the hair at the nape of his neck, and Americo pictures her confronting Carla Bruna in Room 6 at Pleasure Plaza. Two women, gathering for a "special session." He imagines her in the weighty, yellow, decadent light, in the cheap room of the pension, asking her how much she charges, what's the price. He pictures her unbuttoning her blouse, bashful girl, ever so slowly. And Bruna, either suspicious or intrigued, wanting to know if this is her first time. Yes, she confesses, it is. He imagines her reminding herself that she still hasn't taken off her bracelets, her necklace, and going back to the front of the room, to the three-legged bench by the door, where she left her jacket and her purse. He pictures her reaching down into the Italian purse he bought for her, exchanging the jewelry for the knife, concealing it behind her back, and approaching the prostitute, a heat rising into her chest, then up to her neck, her face, her skull, her brain. She surrenders to Queen Carla's embrace; their lips meet. She raises the hand holding the knife. She suffers a split-second of doubt, and then, zip, thrusts the knife into the woman's back. Right in the center of The Bod.

Then she freezes, shocked at the mad simplicity of it all.

The other woman falls on the bed. The brass lamp revolves pitifully over the old carpet. No, this isn't good. This is definitely not good. Joana gawks in horror at her work. Suddenly, a wave of revulsion, an impulse against reality, a desire for blood, a desire to resolve the entire affair in the most definitive way possible, and—*zip, zip*— she stabs the dead woman, slashes her in the chest and on the face, overtaken by an insane ecstasy. She dances in the fresh blood that drips onto the floor, over objects, over memories, just like little drops of virgin olive oil spilling onto a small white dish.

"Everything okay?" asks his wife, peeling off the bed sheets. There's an oblique smile on her face.

Americo looks into her eyes. Two black dots against a blue background. What can he do? Play dumb, act like he knows nothing, fake like he sees nothing in those new eyes of hers? No, the true actor doesn't fake it.

In the film, the final take would show the female lead looking back at us, peering off to the side, trying to peek behind the image, as if mistrusting the camera, the eye that captures everything, the machinery of illusion.

"Don't say a word," he says, squeezing her ass. He slaps her thighs, traces his fingers along her hipbones with the wondrous panic of a little boy learning Braille. *Yes, no.* If he keeps quiet, he's an accomplice. If he advances, he must remain silent forever. *Yes, no, yes, no.* The smell of trees. He remembers what Rosana told him, that to Bruna, he was different, he was special. On the other hand—this bod, here, like this. Such a clear image, the smell of cut trees.

Yes, he'll let it be. He wants this woman in all possible and imaginary ways.

Being Americo Abril.

While they do it, he imagines being watched by bleachers filled with people. The entire country, his mother, his father, his son, friends, secondary characters. They seem happy, moved, like the TV studio audience. Americo turns toward the people in the bleachers and smiles. And they smile back. There are tears of longing, or something like it, in their eyes, but they smile as hard as they can.

It's a happy ending.

About the Translators

JAIME BRAZ was born in 1958 in Luanda, Angola. He has a degree in Biology and teaches at a high school in the Portuguese town of Covilhã, where he lives with his wife, son and dog. His paintings have been exhibited in Portugal and abroad and featured in the Russian edition of *Esquire* magazine. His short fiction has appeared in the *St. Petersburg Review.*

DEAN THOMAS ELLIS is a writer and translator living in New Orleans. His work has appeared in *Bloodroot, Bedtime Stories, St. Petersburg Review, KGB Bar Lit Journal,* and in the online series *Working Stiff* at PBS.org. He hosts the radio programs *Tudo Bem* and *The Dean's List* on WWOZ-FM 90.7 in New Orleans and online at wwoz.org.